prey

You'll want to read these inspiring titles by
Lurlene McDaniel

Angels in Pink
Kathleen's Story • Raina's Story • Holly's Story

One Last Wish novels
Mourning Song • A Time to Die
Mother, Help Me Live • Someone Dies, Someone Lives
Sixteen and Dying • Let Him Live
The Legacy: Making Wishes Come True • Please Don't Die
She Died Too Young • All the Days of Her Life
A Season for Goodbye • Reach for Tomorrow

Other fiction
Hit and Run
Briana's Gift
Letting Go of Lisa
The Time Capsule
Garden of Angels
A Rose for Melinda
Telling Christina Goodbye
How Do I Love Thee: Three Stories
To Live Again
Angel of Mercy • Angel of Hope
Starry, Starry Night: Three Holiday Stories
The Girl Death Left Behind
Angels Watching Over Me
Lifted Up by Angels • Until Angels Close My Eyes
I'll Be Seeing You
Saving Jessica
Don't Die, My Love
Too Young to Die
Goodbye Doesn't Mean Forever
Somewhere Between Life and Death • Time to Let Go
Now I Lay Me Down to Sleep
When Happily Ever After Ends
Baby Alicia Is Dying

From every ending comes a new beginning. . . .

Lurlene McDaniel

DELACORTE PRESS

Published by Delacorte Press
an imprint of Random House Children's Books
a division of Random House, Inc.
New York

This is a work of fiction. Names, characters, places, and incidents
either are the product of the author's imagination or are used fictitiously.
Any resemblance to actual persons, living or dead, events, or locales
is entirely coincidental.

Scripture quotations marked (NIV) are from the Holy Bible, New
International Version. Copyright © 1973, 1978, 1984 by International
Bible Society. Used by permission of Zondervan Bible Publishers.

Visit us on the web! www.randomhouse.com/teens
Educators and librarians, for a variety of teaching tools,
visit us at www.randomhouse.com/teachers

Library of Congress Cataloging-in-Publication Data
McDaniel, Lurlene.
Prey / Lurlene McDaniel. — 1st ed.   p. cm.
Summary: Told from their separate points of view, fifteen-year-old Ryan
has a secret affair with his thirty-three-year-old history teacher at an
Atlanta high school, and his best friend Honey becomes determined to
uncover the reason he is increasingly distant.
ISBN 978-0-385-73453-0 (trade) — ISBN 978-0-385-90457-5 (glb)
[1. Sexual abuse—Fiction. 2. Teachers—Fiction. 3. High schools—Fiction.
4. Schools—Fiction. 5. Interpersonal relations—Fiction. 6. Single-parent
families—Fiction. 7. Fathers and sons—Fiction.]   I. Title.
PZ7.M4784172Pre 2008
[Fic]—dc22   2007012940

The text of this book is set in 11-point Adobe Garamond.
Book design by Vikki Sheatsley
Printed in the United States of America
10 9 8 7 6 5
First Edition

Dedicated to the memory of
Dr. Chris Kiefer and Dr. Jim Parrish,
my teachers and my advocates

The heart is deceitful above all things and beyond cure. Who can understand it?

JEREMIAH 17:9, NIV

A Note from the Author: Part 1

Many of you who are familiar with my work will know that *Prey* is not my typical book. In fact, as it's turned out, it isn't even the book I intended to write about the subject of a female teacher involved with a male high school student. The book I planned was different from this one, but once I got into the research and actual writing of *Prey*, the story took on a life of its own. I hope it makes you come to conclusions, as I did.

This is a novel I felt compelled to write and one that supports my philosophy: no one gets to choose what life gives to him or her; one can only choose how one responds to these happenings. This book is a study of characters who make bad choices, choices that will follow them, even haunt them, for the rest of their lives.

Exploring the issue of relationships between female teachers and male students in a work of fiction has been illuminating, and researching the issue has been both enlightening and disturbing. Here are some facts: no uniform laws govern this issue nationwide—laws differ from state to state. The age of consent varies widely, as do judicial rulings. Punishment is meted out by judges and even juries with few specific guidelines—one state might prosecute harshly, while another might give no more than a slap on the wrist. However, one thing is certain—the number of these cases, or at least the reporting of them, is growing in our schools, both public and private.

PART
1

Ryan

Day one. New school year. New school. Freshman status. Same old Ryan Piccoli. Me, myself and I, lost in the masses—heading to new classes, new teachers, new everything. This is the thing about big high schools like McAllister. People can look right at you, right through you, as if you're Casper the Friendly Ghost.

"Hey, watch where you're going, turd."

I've bumped into a senior, a jock, and he's snarling at me. I bow slightly and get out of his way. He'd stopped without warning in the middle of the hall. I say, "Sorry, my bad. I didn't see the traffic light over your head giving you the right of way." His pretty girlfriend looks me over, giggles.

The guy puffs up. "Take off, creep."

He turns and I take a chance and wink at his girlfriend. She's pretty, but off-limits.

She blows me a kiss when her boyfriend isn't

looking and I watch them take off down the crowded hallway. Wait for it, I think, and am rewarded when she glances over her shoulder to make sure I'm still watching. Gotcha!

I can make people like me, even when they don't want to. A talent that got me through middle school—just ask my teachers. If you can't make them love you, make them like you. How, you ask? Make 'em laugh. A survival skill I learned early in life.

I'm wishing the day was ending instead of just starting. My summer was pretty laid-back, sleeping in and staying up until three in the morning on my computer. I hung at the pool at the country club, worked on my tan, lifted weights in my garage every afternoon. For a freshman nobody, I look pretty good. At least that's what some girls hanging at the pool said. Sure, they were only eleven and twelve, but girls' opinions are always worth something to me. With school starting up, though, talking to the global universe and gaming are over.

"Ry! Wait up."

I turn and see Joel weaving through the hall traffic. When he reaches me, he asks, "You home this afternoon?" He'd been a regular drop-by at my place through middle school. My dad's in sales and he travels a lot, so except for a housekeeper now and then, I'm pretty much on my own most days of the week.

"As soon as the bus drops me," I say.

"Forget the bus. I'll give you a lift."

Joel's had a car since July. I won't turn sixteen until December and that's when I hope Dad will get me a car. Until then, I'm at the mercy of the school bus and a few friends who have their own wheels. "All right," I tell him. "I got the new Grand Slam Poker game on Saturday."

Joel's eyes light up. "I'm in."

"It's tricky."

"Bring it on. You're lucky your dad gets you stuff like that. I have to save every cent and buy stuff I want myself."

Lucky? I think. It's a bribe, Joel, my man. Dad buys me stuff because he sheds guilt over leaving me alone so much like a shaggy dog sheds hair. His guilt is my ticket to the latest and greatest. A guy adapts.

The foot traffic in the hall has thinned and the first bell buzzes. "I'm gone," I say, waving my schedule.

"Wait by the gym," Joel calls, and takes off in the other direction.

My first class is World History from Ancient to Modern Times, and by the time I get there, all the seats in the back of the room are taken. I find an empty one in the middle of the third row and slide into it, curling my legs. Man, these things must be left over from some elementary school. The room smells of chalk dust and stale air. All schools smell the same.

If someone blindfolded you and led you through a maze ending in a classroom, you'd know in an instant where you were by the smells.

The door shuts and a woman's voice says, "Welcome to WHAM—your free pass to Tomorrow Land. I'm Ms. Settles."

I look up because I can feel an undercurrent flowing through the room. I hear the guy next to me exhale a soft "wow."

Ms. Settles is gorgeous. Straight jet-black hair to her shoulders, skin the color of cream and big blue eyes so clear you could swim in them. Her body is as sexy as any movie star's, with curves and boobs and a sweaterdress that shows off her assets.

"H-e-l-l-o, Ms. Settles," a guy on the other side of me whispers.

The girls in the class are speechless. Probably because none of them look like that, poor slobs.

Ms. Settles is all business, walking down each aisle, her heels clicking, talking about history—who cares? When she passes me, I catch a whiff of vanilla and see that she has nails painted pale icy pink, perfectly rounded and shiny.

In front of her desk again, she leans backward, resting her palms on the desktop and crossing her ankles. She isn't wearing athletic shoes, or old lady loafers either. Her shoes are black and high, with ankle straps that show off her smooth, tanned and perfect calves. She never stops talking about world history, her voice professional-sounding, but who can listen? I just keep seeing how pretty she is.

She asks two guys to go to the back cabinet and pass out the textbooks. They about fall over themselves to get it done. The thick blue book lands with a thud on my desk and I thumb through it. All the while Ms. Settles is outlining her program, test schedule and essay work for the school year. I hardly hear her words, just her voice. Pretty voice, too.

Then she starts asking questions. "Who in here thinks history is a waste of time?" Silence. "Who thinks the past is dead, so why bother studying it? Who thinks hard work equals good grades?" More silence. "Who thinks he or she can slide by because they're only doing time at McAllister, waiting for better things to come along?" Feet shuffle. She's speaking in teacher code, letting us know that her class isn't going to be a walk in the park. "This is my first year here, but I've taught middle and high school for over seven years."

I do rapid math and calculate her age to be thirty-ish if she graduated college at twenty-two. She's old. So what? She's still jaw-dropping delectable.

She asks, "Who can name one famous historian for me?"

Pages rustle as a few kids leaf through their books. Do they think the answer will pop out at them? I feel my mouth go dry and before I can stop myself I say aloud, "Me and Noah."

All heads turn my way. Ms. Settles' blue eyes grab hold of mine. "Noah?" she says.

I gain confidence with everyone looking at me. I shrug and give her my best grin. "Yeah. I know a lot of reasons to love history."

Kids laugh. Others groan at my sorry play on words. It breaks the silence in the room, though. People look back at Ms. Settles to see how she'll react. She raises a perfect eyebrow. "And your name, sir?"

"Ryan Piccoli. No disrespect, Ms. Settles."

Our eyes stay locked and it's as if she's seeing inside my head. I feel heat.

"And," she says, "I know a lot of reasons why you should sit up here in the first seat right in front of my desk."

Now everybody laughs. She's turned the tables and is showing us she can be a good sport. I hop up, grab my books and grin all the way to the vacant desk immediately in front of hers. Three guys give me high fives as I walk by. A few of the girls give me sullen stares. The girls look like babies to me compared with Ms. Settles.

Just then, the bell sounds and Ms. Settles calls out

the assignment. I scoop up my books and head for the door, turning once to see her bending over the open bottom drawer of her desk. The sweaterdress hugs her backside, and I want to do the same. I leave the room before the impulse gets the best of me.

Honey

I see Ryan coming toward me down the hall and my stomach does its fish-flopping-on-dry-land routine. He's gorgeous, sexy and intelligent—a smart-aleck and a flirt, but I forgive him all his faults. My friend since fourth grade. Never to be my boyfriend. It sucks, but a girl knows these things. She might not like it, but she knows.

"Hey, Honey." He greets me with that flirty smile of his. My name is Honey Fowler, an amazingly stupid choice of a name by my parents that I've suffered with for years. There's nothing cute, cuddly or honey-ish about me. My parents had been wowed by a character in some police drama on TV with the name Honey, so that's what they named me. Thanks, scriptwriters of the eighties.

"Hey yourself." I cradle my books and stand out of the way of the hall foot traffic. "How was your first day?"

"Same old. How about you?"

I'm in honors classes, where Ryan could be if he'd take school more seriously. "It's going to be harder this year."

"If anyone can do it, it's you."

I love basking in his attention. "So what's up today?"

"Joel's picking me up and we're going to my place for some thumb exercises."

"A new video game? No homework?"

"Don't nag." He waggles his finger at me.

"You seen the new teacher?"

Now his grin widens. "Seen her! I have her. Academically speaking, of course. World history."

I'd seen her in the lunchroom, where every male in the place leered when she walked through to buy ice tea. I guess they were out of tea in the faculty lounge. "Please don't say obvious things about taking a tour of her body."

"I'm crushed that you would even think me so shallow and insensitive." He widens blue eyes, feigning innocence. "It doesn't have to be an entire tour, you know."

I slug his arm. "You're bad to the bone, Piccoli." Then I add, "I think she looks like a hooker." It's mean, but teachers should wear cute baggy sweaters and not flaunt their bodies.

"I think she looks hot," he says. "Not your usual female for a high school faculty."

I feel my face turn red. To me, his saying that means I am not hot. "But she's supposed to teach, not look hot."

"She can't do both?"

I'm digging a hole for myself but don't know how to get out of it.

"You going to the game Friday night?" Ryan changes the subject.

"Probably."

"Then sit with me and Joel."

His magic smile appears again and I melt. "Jessica and Taylor will be with me."

"That's fine."

"Then okay." I shrug, knowing that our time together for today is over. I long for the days of elementary when Ryan would come home with me after school and we'd spend the afternoon together climbing trees and building forts. I was a pretty good dragon slayer in those days. Now all I'm good for is basketball. I'm the center, and I make a good one because I'm so tall. Another un-honeylike trait.

"I'm out of here," he says, and I watch him take off. By now the halls are empty and I know I've missed my bus. Mom's not going to be thrilled about coming to pick me up, either. I retrieve my cell from my locker and dial her up.

"Oh, Honey . . . how'd you miss the bus?" She sounds irritated.

"First day and all," I say. "Tons of confusion. Sorry."

She sighs. "I have to pull Cory away from his TV shows."

"I said I was sorry." My nine-year-old brother, Cory, is autistic. Not bad autistic, but enough to be a problem. Kids like him love ritual, and breaking his routines can mean a tantrum.

"Where should I meet you?"

"Out front. No hurry. Let Cory watch the rest of his show. There's a bench and I can sit and read."

"I'll be there soon as I can."

We hang up and I go outside. I hate being fifteen. Too young to drive without some adult in the car with me. Too old to ride the stupid school bus and feel good about myself. I think of Ryan again. One more thing I can't have. I should start a list.

Lori

*N*ever let them see you sweat. The old sports adage is my first thought as my classroom fills up with young bodies. New faces turn to each other; they ignore the room and me, and all the work I've put into making it student friendly, smart, not too schoolroom-ish. I check them over as they come inside—tall ones, short ones, pretty ones and the not-so-pretty, the ones with skin scarred by acne and the overweight, the shy, the loud, the teases—all fresh in their youth and vitality, unable to see what they possess simply by being young. I envy them. And I'm drawn to them. I covet their innocence, their youth.

I became a teacher because I wanted to make a difference in kids' lives. A simple objective. But it is they, the students, who over time have made a difference in mine. I watch a girl settle into a front-row chair. She'll be a studious type, eager to please and make good grades. In the back, a row of boys—big, gangly boys—plops down. They're probably of the "I hate school" mentality, and hunch over their desks, some already dozing off, too bored to care. First-period classes suck. Research shows that teenagers don't really wake up until midmorning. They come alive at night, when their parents are sacked out.

I come alive at night too.

The bell rings and I introduce myself, begin my spiel about world history ancient and modern. Their eyes take me in, sweeping me with expressions that ask, "Is she for real?" It's what I want from them, what I've come to expect. They won't forget me, of that I'm sure. I ask for texts to be passed around. A few of the males fall over themselves to comply.

I stand in front of my desk for effect, the old oak surface rough and pitted against my hands. Not like at the private school where I last taught. There the furniture was smooth and polished, dark with age and prestige. I ask my series of questions to the upturned faces. The class sits mutely, staring. My psyche sinks. Ordinary. How can they all be so ordinary?

Then one speaks out. A wise-guy answer that makes the room laugh. He's beautiful. Dark hair, blue eyes, dimples—not yet a man, yet more than a child. Yes, I know that too in an instant. It's a gift, being able to see inside them. I stare at him and the room seems to recede. A halo of light encircles him and suddenly, I know . . . he'll be the One.

Ryan

Dad comes in Thursday evening from his road trip. He sells hospital equipment—big, expensive, one-of-a-kind units. His territory is the East Coast, and his typical week is out Monday morning and back home to Atlanta on Thursday. He's hired us a housekeeper, who cleans once a week, and she has a sister he pays to cook us meals ahead of time and freeze them so we never go hungry. Plus, we never have to cook.

"How's school?" Dad asks.

He starts all our conversations this way.

"Fine." And I answer this way, but he never seems to notice the sameness.

"Any good classes?"

Sure, he calls home when he's gone, but just to check in, make sure nothing major has gone wrong. He doesn't know about any of my new classes yet. He doesn't know about Ms. Settles—Lori's her first name.

What should I tell him? That she's a babe? That I sit in front of her desk every day and drool? That I watch her every move? Her legs are long, and she always wears heels that make them look even longer. Sometimes when I see her unexpectedly, like in the halls or in the lunchroom, my heart races and the crotch of my pants gets tight.

"Classes are all right. A lot more homework than last year," I tell him, because I have to say something, and I sure don't feel like telling him about Lori Settles.

"Any of your friends in your classes?"

"Joel has English in the same room as me, but in the next period."

"That's it?"

I'm not making it easy for him, but I really don't want to talk. I've got a load of homework waiting upstairs. Besides, Dad and I have never been good at small talk.

"Any girls?"

He's asked me that every year since seventh grade. It irks me. "I have girls in every class except phys ed. Rules, you know."

"Don't be smart. You know what I mean. Any girls that look good to you?"

"Shouldn't you ask if I look good to any girls? I'm not exactly a babe magnet."

He gives me a long stare and I wait for his usual comeback: "Why not? You got my good looks."

He says, "Sure you are . . . what with my good looks in your DNA."

Predictable. He doesn't mention my mother. He never does. It's as if he found me in the backyard or something. As if I were an asexual experiment. I don't think much about my mom these days. I used to when I was a kid, but no more. Too much going on to think about that now.

"Anything happening this weekend?"

"Game tomorrow night. I'm going with Joel. In his car," I add pointedly.

Dad ignores my transportation hint and begins to shuffle through the mail Mrs. Gomez has stacked on the table for him. "Have fun."

"You around next week?" I ask.

"Off to Richmond on Sunday."

I watch him sort the mail and I know I've been dismissed. I leave him and go up to my room. Welcome home, Dad.

Honey

The entire ride to the football game Friday night is spent talking about the new teacher, Lori Settles. I sit in the backseat and listen to Jessica and Taylor trash the woman. Not that I want to defend her. She really isn't the typical teacher, and for some reason, it bothers me. And not because she wears heels and body-hugging clothes every day.

"Stilettos?" Jess asks, and I know she's rolling her eyes. "Who wears stilettos to teach history?" She also has world history with Ms. Settles, but fifth period.

"Well, nobody's mind wanders," Taylor says. "Not the guys' minds, at least."

"Oh, their minds wander, all right," Jess says. "Just not to history."

They laugh. Taylor, in the front passenger seat, turns to look at me. "You're awful quiet. Do you like Stiletto Settles?"

"I haven't met her, but I hear all the guys talking,"

I tell her. My mind is more on catching up to Ryan at the game. We've exchanged some e-mails. He thinks Settles is smoking hot. Of course. He's a red-blooded male.

"The best thing to come out of Settles' arrival is that now the focus is off Jordan Leslie."

Jordan is captain of our cheerleaders: blond, pretty and always at the top of the lust list of the boys now talking about Settles. She's thought of herself as a princess ever since sixth grade, and none of us like her. Not that she cares, because my friends and I will never register on the babe Richter scale, so we're of no interest to her or her little followers and worshipers.

"True," Jess says. "She was pouting, I heard, because Lars said Ms. Settles was giving him wet dreams." Lars is Jordan's boyfriend.

"A well-groomed collie could give him wet dreams," I say, and the others laugh hard.

We park in a crowded lot next to the field and walk to the stands, already full of students. I look for Ryan, but covertly, because I don't want Taylor and Jess to know. When I see him, my heartbeat picks up. He's sitting with Joel, sees us and waves.

"Ryan's saved us some space," I tell my friends. "That was nice of him." They exchange glances, but the cheerleaders finish a routine and the whole bleacher erupts into yowls, drowning out any comments Jess and Taylor might make. They know I've had a thing for Ryan for years, even though I don't talk about it.

"Hey," Ryan says, moving his stuff aside so we can sit. Joel ogles Jess.

I sit next to Ryan, hoping no one can guess that my heart is thudding like a drum. "Think we can win this one?" I ask.

"Only if their quarterback drops dead during the coin toss," Ryan says.

Joel nudges Ryan and says, "Whoa! Look at that."

Lori Settles is passing below us along the bleachers. Her black hair is tied back and she's wearing a ballcap, a suede jacket and skintight jeans.

"Makes my knees weak," Joel says.

"Isn't she wearing stilettos?" Jess asks snidely.

"Boots," Ryan says, following her with his eyes. "Baby-blue cowboy boots. Would you look at that."

The expression on Ryan's face tells me that's not all he's noticing. Her jeans follow the curve of her butt like a second skin, and Ryan sweeps her backside in one long admiring look. Behind us, someone whistles. Someone else shouts, "Bring it on home to me, baby." Shushing and laughing everywhere. Settles appears to hear nothing. My mouth tastes sour. What I wouldn't give to have Ryan look at me that way. But he won't. I'm too big and horsey. I'm not pretty. I'm plain and ordinary. I'm just a girl he's known for years.

Jess leans over and whispers in my ear. "She's out of his league."

I start, feel color rise to my cheeks. My pathetic thoughts must be written on my face. I glance at Jess, see understanding. "And he's out of mine," I say.

A whistle blows and both football teams run onto the field. The stands on both sides of the field go crazy. My moment of unmasking passes, and I stand and shout for our team, pouring all my frustration into it.

Ryan

I like sitting in front of her desk, doodling in my notebook and mentally undressing her. Her lectures are all business, but when she moves, my mouth waters. Okay, so I have the hots for my teacher. It's not the first time. My "love" was purer, but when I was in kindergarten, I loved Mrs. Knobler. In first grade, I fell hard for Mrs. Rubinstein. When I hit second grade and found out I wouldn't be in her room again, I had a meltdown. Dad took me to some shrink who talked to me endlessly and told Dad I was "projecting" and turning women who remained consistent in my life into "mother figures" because I had no mother. What a bunch of crap. There's nothing about Ms. Settles that makes me wish for a mother.

Three weeks into the school year, Ms. Settles asks me if I could come to her room after the last bell and I about fall over myself, telling her yes even though it means missing the school bus and having to take two city buses to get home. The rest of the day drags. I look at the wall clocks fifty times, wishing time away. When the day is finally officially over, I saunter back to her room, forcing myself not to hurry so that I don't get there out of breath from having run all the way.

The halls are almost empty by the time I arrive. She's sitting at her desk reading papers. She looks up, smiles. "Ryan. Thank you for coming."

"Not a problem," I say.

"Good."

She leans back in the chair and I can't keep my eyes to myself. They just help themselves to a long stare at her perfect body.

"Ryan, do you know a couple of young men who might be willing to help me move furniture?"

I swallow. My mind races over a short list of my friends. "What kind of furniture?"

She laughs and the sound is soft and silky. "Let me better explain. You see, I took this job at McAllister at the last minute and moved down from Chicago quickly. Then I had to be here getting things ready for the new year a week in advance of classes. Then classes started, and, well, I've never really unpacked my stuff. The movers just dumped my furniture in my apartment, and I'm tired of walking around it. Every piece needs placement. I can't move it by myself and I don't know a soul in Atlanta. So I thought maybe I could hire a few of my students to help me move the pieces I want to reposition."

I nod almost the whole time she's talking. "Sure, sure. I know some guys."

"I'll pay all of you well."

I feel giddy. "When did you want to do this?"

"Saturday morning? About ten-thirty?" she asks so sweetly that I almost beg her to start right now.

"Sounds good to me."

"You're a lifesaver. I'd hate for you to miss out on any other plans you've made, so I promise we'll do this quickly. I already know where I want everything." She looks at me through long dark lashes. "You sure you don't mind?"

"No problem."

She smiles brightly. "That's such a relief. I can't tell you how much I appreciate this."

She grabs a legal pad and writes down her address.

I reach for the pad.

"Wait," she says. "Let me write down my cell number too. If something goes wrong, if you can't come, just let me know."

I would have shown up even if it meant canceling an audience with the Pope. I take the pad and tear off the paper, fold it and slide it into the pocket of my jeans. "See you Saturday," I say.

"Yes. And thank you again."

I leave her and scoot down the empty hall, knowing

I have to move fast because the resource cop locks the doors at four. At the bus stop, I remove and unfold the paper from my pocket. I read her address and phone number in her neat handwriting and my palms get sweaty. I don't know where her apartment is in the city, but I'll download a map tonight. I think about who I'll ask to come with me. Joel's the logical choice. Yet something inside me doesn't want him to come. I don't even want him to know. I don't want anyone to know. Me and Lori Settles moving furniture. How lucky can one guy get?

On Saturday I make up some story for Dad about meeting kids from my science class at a coffee shop that's around the corner from Lori Settles' apartment complex. The Internet is helpful for finding all kinds of info—so I know exactly where she lives and what's near her apartment. I drive and Dad rides in the passenger seat. He's been letting me drive since before I got my learner's permit, but he still won't let me take the car on my own. Not until I'm sixteen. I feel like such a kid and make my case again for my own wheels as a Christmas gift.

"I get it, Ryan," he says once I rehash my reasons. "I get it every time you ask."

"But you never tell me if it's going to happen."

"Have you figured a way to pay for insurance and gas? Cars are expensive to keep, you know."

"I'll get a job. The grocery store always needs baggers."

"You've got to keep your grades up."

"I'll do it."

He sighs, runs his hand through his thinning hair. "Well, stop badgering me. I've got a lot on my mind."

"Work?"

"Always. Some hotshot from the home office wants to intrude on my sales territory."

"Can he?"

"I have seniority, but you never know."

The equipment he sells is state of the art. He only has to sell a few a year for his commission to cover our expenses, but he has to keep customers happy and that's why he travels so much. He handholds and troubleshoots for every piece of equipment he sells. "I'm sure you can take him, Dad."

That makes Dad laugh. "Thanks for the vote of confidence."

I pull up to the curb in front of the coffee shop, grab a paper sack from the backseat and get out of the car.

"Where's your notebook?" he asks.

"Girls take notes. Guys bring lunch."

He laughs again. "I'll give you a few bucks for lunch." He hands me a ten, a bonus for the little lie I've told so smoothly. "You have a time frame for me?"

"I don't know how long this is going to take."

"You can call—"

"I'll hitch a ride with one of the guys," I say. "That way you can do what needs doing in your life."

"You sure?"

"Positive." I've already plotted my bus route home, and Dad'll never know how I actually get there.

He drives off and I enter the coffee shop in case he's looking in the rearview mirror. As soon as I think it's safe, I leave the shop, head over to the next block and to the giant complex Lori Settles calls home. My heart is thudding and my mouth is dry. I can't wait to get started.

Ryan

Lori Settles lives in building five on floor five of the Garden Ridge apartments, overlooking Georgia pines, oaks and maple trees. I ring her doorbell. When she opens the door, she's wearing tight jeans, a body-hugging hot pink T-shirt and a smile. "Ryan, come in." She crooks her neck to look past me into the empty hallway. "Where are the others?"

I flash my best grin. "Just me. All my buds were covered up."

"But the furniture's heavy."

I hold up the paper sack I've brought with me and shake it. "I have other friends." I reach into the bag and pull out four padded disks with slick surfaces. "These are called 'moving men.' You slide them under the feet of the furniture you need moved and push, and presto—instant move, no effort. These babies and two people can move the world."

She stares at the disks, then returns my smile. "Then let's get started."

She walks into the living room. Her black hair is tied back with a pink velvet ribbon and she's wearing lip gloss that makes her mouth look slick and pouty. I feel like a slobbery dog as I follow her.

"Well, here it is," she says, gesturing at stacks of boxes and several large pieces of furniture along the walls.

"This one first," I say, pointing to a large cabinet that I'm guessing holds dishes; the one at our house does. "Where do you want it?"

"Over there." She points to a wall near a kitchen pass-through.

"All you have to do is help me tip it," I say. "I'll do the rest." I drop to my knees and put the pads directly under the furniture's front legs while she tips the cabinet up. We repeat the process for the back legs. Then I slide the heavy unit effortlessly across the carpet while she guides it.

Lori claps when it's in place. "How easy! You're a genius."

I beam at the sound of her praise. "What's next?"

We finish the living room and dining room in record time, stopping only to shuffle stacks of boxes out of the way. I'm thinking that she has a lot of stuff, but then I remember she's had years to collect it.

Everything I own fits into my fourteen-by-twelve-foot bedroom.

Once she tells me she's happy with where we've put the furniture, she says, "Let's take a break. Do you like cappuccino?"

"Sure." I'd have drunk cat pee if she'd offered it. "I saw a coffee shop on my way here."

She laughs. "I have a machine in the kitchen, silly."

I feel my face get red but follow her into the kitchen. The machine sits on the counter, and I watch her every move as she makes the coffee.

"Sit," she says, and I grab a chair at a small round table in the corner. "I worked at Starbucks in college," she says. "I can do this with my eyes closed."

The coffee smells great and tastes even better. I tell her so.

"You don't have to call me Ms. Settles when we're off campus," she says. "I'm Lori."

This makes me feel special. "I promise not to forget when we're on school property," I say.

"You better not, or I'll give you a detention."

Her eyes sparkle and I know she's teasing. It's hard to look away, but I do. "I don't have to be anywhere else, so I can work all day."

"Really?" She sets her cup down and her hand brushes mine. It feels like an electric shock shooting through me. We both jerk away. She laughs. "Static electricity."

Maybe so. But my heart's pounding like a drum and every nerve in my body is jangling. I jump up from the table. "What's next?"

She looks at me levelly. "Why, my bedroom, of course."

Honey

I'm bummed out because Ryan's a no-show. On the third Saturday of every month, I take my brother to the library for story hour. It gets Cory out of the house and gives him exposure to the real world, and it gives Mom a break. Ryan rarely misses meeting us there. We've done this together for years. He can handle Cory if he gets unruly, plus Cory likes both Ryan and story hour. When I talked to Ryan at school on Friday, he said he'd be at the library, but he isn't.

After I settle Cory in the reading room with the other kids, I call Ryan's cell. No answer. I leave a message, hoping I don't sound whiny or hurt or mad, which I am—all of the above. Next I call his home and his dad answers.

"I dropped him off at some coffee shop to meet with some kids from his science class about ten this morning."

I know this is totally bogus. Ryan would have told

me about any science project. "Um—oh yes, I forgot about that." I hate myself for covering for him, but I do it anyway.

"You tried his cell?"

"He didn't answer."

"I'll tell him you called."

We hang up and I slide into a blue funk. Where is he? Why has he blown off me and Cory? Even though he'll never see me as anything more than a gal-pal, I see him as the world's most perfect male specimen. It's the dark hair and blue eyes and thousand-watt smile. It's his wit and charm and sense of humor. It's him. Totally him that lights my fire.

I call Jessica. "Want to hit a movie this afternoon?"

"Hey, you sound down. What's the prob?"

The girl must have radar. "Just stuck at the library for Miss Ethel's Story Hour. The woman's dressed up like Mother Goose. Gag me."

"Isn't Ryan with you?"

"Not today."

"And that explains why Honey's unhappy. Did he bail?"

No use protesting the obvious with Jess. "He didn't come. He didn't call."

"You've got to get over him, girlfriend."

"Why? Maybe I'm addicted to pain and frustration."

"Then you should be medicated."

That makes me laugh. "Can we go to a movie or not?"

"We can go. Call me when you get home from story hour."

I feel better after talking to Jess, and punch off. I hear loud voices coming from the reading room and I run toward them. Inside, Cory is having a tantrum, kicking and screaming on the floor. I rush over and lift him, get behind him and lock my arms and legs around him. He struggles, but he can't move. I know he hates being pinned in place, but I don't have a choice. He can't be reasoned with when he gets this way. "Call our mother," I say to a librarian.

Kids have scattered like ants and are in little huddles, watching Cory wide-eyed. I get angry at Ryan all over again. He should have been here to help. He said he would be, but he isn't. So where is he?

Lori

I'm alone now. All my furniture is in place and the beautiful boy is gone. He lingered, dragging out the time it took him to do the job. I'm pleased about that. Everything about him pleases me. He wanted so much to impress me, to make me see him as strong and manly. And I do.

The pure sweetness of him makes me feel warm inside. The adoring glances he threw my way all afternoon. Not like the lecherous stares of grown men. I hate the way they look at me, as if they want to tear my clothes off. The jerks. Not like the young ones, who long to touch but don't.

I look at my hand, at the place where our fingers touched and sparks flew. I smile. How tender and dear that moment. The heart-pounding part came when I took him into my bedroom. He looked scared, then curious, as he crossed the threshold.

I said, "I'm thinking the bed should go on this

wall. That way when I wake up in the morning, I can look straight out that window at the tops of the trees and the sky behind them. Good idea?"

"Y-yes. Good plan."

His voice is hesitant, as if a woman has never asked his opinion on anything. Together we struggle with the queen-size mattress, standing it on end to better move the bedframe. When the frame is in place, we tug the mattress onto it. For a moment, I think about letting him help me make the bed, but decide it's too soon. We move the dresser next, then my jewelry box, a large piece of furniture made of dark wood.

"I really hate to put my computer desk in here," I say. "Bedrooms shouldn't be used for work, but I really don't know where else to put my computer— you know, the lesson planning and bill paying."

He puckers his brow and I can tell he's really thinking through my dilemma. "Maybe you can figure a way to hide it. Like a screen or something."

"Why, Ryan, that's brilliant! How clever of you."

My words make him blush. I love seeing his skin turn pink and his eyes shine. The boy is starved for approval. I wonder about his parents, his mother especially. In time I'll get him to tell me about his family. Not today.

I look around the room. "I guess that's about it. I shouldn't keep you any longer."

"It's no problem."

"Oh, go have fun. It's Saturday." I smile, walk out my bedroom door. He has no choice except to follow.

In the living room, I pick up my purse. "Let me pay you."

"That's all right. You don't need—"

"Of course I do. I promised." I extract two twenties from my wallet and hand them over.

"That's too much."

"Well, don't forget, you have to pay the moving men."

He looks blank; then a smile spreads across his face. "I'll take them to the mall, buy them a meal."

We laugh at his joke.

"Thank you, Ryan. You're a lifesaver."

His eyes linger on mine and I sense his willingness to do anything I ask. My breath quickens. The timing's wrong. I open the door. "See you Monday."

"Sure, Ms. Settles." He slides back into being my student.

"And one more thing." He pauses and I give him a most important instruction. He nods and agrees.

I close the door behind him, hoping he'll keep his word.

Ryan

My friends are pissed at me. Honey and Joel both.
I feel bad about missing the library gig
with Honey and Cory, especially when I hear that
Cory went postal over something that only his brain
can grasp. That's the thing about autism: no one can
get inside Cory's head and see the world through his
eyes, so we never know what sets him off. It just happens, so the main goal is to keep him from hurting
himself until his brain wiring trips him back into our
universe. I apologize all over myself and Honey says
she understands and that I don't have to show up for
Cory outings, but because I said I would, she was
counting on me. I feel her disappointment vibes like
arrows.

I can't tell her what I was really doing—moving
furniture at Lori's place—even though Honey leaves
me openings as wide as the freeway to spill my secrets

into. The story about a science project is too lame to even repeat, so I tell her nothing, cling to loyalty toward Lori.

The last thing Lori said to me was "Ryan, I think it best if we kept this little adventure to ourselves. Will you do that, please?"

I had just spent an hour moving furniture around her bedroom and the rough feel of the wood was still on my hands, and the scent of her perfume was still in my nose. I told her, "You don't have to worry about that," although now every cell in my body wants to shout it out to Joel. To anyone who'll listen.

Joel's mad at me too, but for different reasons than not helping Honey on Saturday. Joel's mad because on Thursday, I tell him I won't be a part of the freshman male idiot squad at Friday night's football game.

"But we planned doing this all summer," he says. "At the pool. We talked about it with Ray and Steve. They're counting on us."

We're in my garage and I'm doing some free weights to bulk up my chest and arms. "Plans change."

"You're not going to the game?"

"No, I'm going. I'm just not stripping to my waist, painting myself half orange and half blue and standing in the bleachers cheering for our lousy team. Do you know how cold it's supposed to get by tomorrow night?" I drop the barbells with a thud onto the mat in the corner where I've set up my gym.

"So what? Ten guys are doing it," Joel says, as if the herd mentality will make me change my mind.

"Then have fun. And don't let your tits freeze."

"Every freshman class does it at the final home game of the year. It's a tradition."

"So is hari-kari, but I'm not going there."

Joel's mad. "What's gotten into you? You're not acting like yourself."

"Why? Because I don't want to get half naked and act like an ass? Well, I don't."

Joel is quiet for a minute. He blurts out, "It's a girl, isn't it? You're trying to impress some girl and don't want her to see you doing this."

I turn so that he can't see my face and how close to the mark he's come. I know Lori goes to the games, and he's right. I don't want her to see me as I am— fifteen, ages younger than her. "Yeah, I'm a real babe magnet," I say to Joel. "Don't you see them line up at my locker every morning?"

He stares.

I say, "Look, is this going to kill our friendship?"

He shrugs. "Course not. I just thought we'd do this together because we talked about it so much. We thought it would be fun."

"You don't have to do this either, you know."

"No. I said I would. I won't let the guys down."

Every word drips with implication about my values as far as friendship is concerned. "Then see you tomorrow night—if it won't embarrass you to speak."

Joel walks to his car, peels out of my driveway. I watch him go without regrets. He needs to chill. And grow up.

Lori—Ms. Settles in the classroom—treats me . . . well, I'm not sure. Some days I think she looks right through me. Other times, her eyes connect with mine and I go hot all over. I think about going to her room after school. I think about asking, "So how's the new furniture arrangement working for you?" Sometimes during class I goof off, say a few things that make the kids in the room laugh. She often smiles too, but quickly puts on her teacher face and tells me to settle down.

Right before Halloween, she makes an announcement to the whole class. "Look, if any of you would like something to do this Saturday, the Fulton firefighters are sponsoring a carnival and pumpkin sale at Centennial Park. One of the firemen lives in my complex and his wife asked me if I knew of any teens who might be interested in volunteering to help. I said I'd ask my classes." Hands shoot up. Not mine. Ms. Settles smiles. "If you can come, show up Saturday morning at eight in the park. I really appreciate your willingness to help. And it's all right if you can't come. It's just a nice thing to do."

I swear she looks right at me when she says this. If I can't come. Wild horses couldn't keep me away.

Joel drives me and Honey and Jessica to the park. I think Joel has a thing for Jess, but I don't ride him because he's still honked at me for bailing on the football game/body painting fiasco. I don't care. I kept my dignity.

At the park we join up with an assembly of kids from Ms. Settles' world history classes. I'm surprised at how many showed up. "Butt kissers," Honey whispers.

"So why did you come? You're not even in any of her classes."

Honey blushes. "Duh . . . to get out of cleaning the house."

I grin. "And I thought it was to do a good deed."

"That too."

A fireman comes over and gives a spiel about what's going on, offers us choices of where we can work for the day. I notice that he can't keep his eyes off Lori. Why should he? She's dressed in jeans, black boots and a black turtleneck with a wow factor of ten plus.

I choose to help kids at a game where they catch magnetic fish in a dry wading pool for prizes. Honey tags along. After about fifteen minutes, I've taken a ton of fish off the magnets and Honey's passed out a ton of cheap prizes. I say, "We should have brought Cory. He'd love this."

"Mom wanted me to bring him, but I didn't want to spend my time watching him. What if he went off like he did at the library?"

She's never going to let me forget how I let her down. We work for an hour and I decide to go grab us some hot chocolate at the concession tent. I'm in line when a voice from behind me asks, "Having fun, Ryan?"

I turn to see Lori. The smoothness of her voice and the way she says my name make my heart trip. "Sure."

"I didn't think you'd come," she says.

I shrug. "Why not? I had nothing else going today."

She smiles. "I appreciate so many of my students giving up their Saturday to help others. It's kind of you."

"I guess I'm in the habit of giving up my Saturdays for you, Ms. Settles."

She arches one perfect eyebrow. "Not a burden, I hope."

I should have kept my mouth shut. The last thing I want to do is offend her, but sharing cappuccino in her kitchen, moving her possessions, was good stuff for me. I want her to think of me not as just some kid in her class. "I'd do it again," I say. "Anytime."

She hugs her arms to her body, gives me her teacher smile—an adult passing time with a student. "So the girl who came with you today—is she your girlfriend?"

"Honey? No way. We've been friends since grade school. I don't have a girlfriend."

She looks as if she doesn't believe me. "How can that be? I would have thought you had several."

"I'm holding out for the right one to come along."

Now she laughs. "You're a romantic boy. When I went to high school, with guys it was 'If you're not with the girl you love, then love the girl you're with.'"

I don't like her calling me a boy. I don't like thinking about how many years separate us. "Well, that's not me," I say.

Her eyes go soft. "Good for you. Hold out."

Somebody says, "Could you close the gap there, buddy?"

I start, look around and see that I'm holding up the concession line. I push forward and Lori comes with me. "I'll be scheduling parent-teacher visits in a week. I'm looking forward to meeting your family." She's all teacher again. "They are planning on coming, aren't they?"

"My dad will show," I say.

"Not your mother?"

"No." I turn, leaving her to wonder, to be curious the way I'm curious why she comes on to me one minute and retreats the next. I've never known a teacher like her. A teacher who runs hot and cold. Maybe it's just a girl thing.

Honey

I get tired of waiting for Ryan to show with my hot chocolate. He's been gone forever and the sun's disappeared behind clouds and the temperature's dropping. I pass out a few more prizes and ask some girl to take my place. "Potty break," I tell her.

I trot to the concession tent and duck inside. Since my heart has automatic radar for him, it takes my eyes about fifteen seconds to locate him in the crowd. He's standing off to one side holding two paper cups and talking to Ms. Settles. It bothers me.

"What's eating you?"

It's Jess, who's come up beside me. "Nothing."

"That's not what your face is saying."

I look at Jess. "Ryan went to get us hot chocolate and got waylaid by Stiletto Settles."

We look across the tent together.

"They're just talking," Jess says. "Besides, she's okay. I like her."

"Oh, so now you're her defense attorney? A few weeks ago, you were calling her names."

"Things change. She's all right. Really."

"Oh, please!"

"Whoa! Why are you getting so worked up?"

I ignore her, march to the back of the concession line. She follows. "I'm thirsty. And cold. He was supposed to be right back."

Jess takes my arm. "Slow down, Honey. You're acting jealous. She's a teacher, girl, and tons older than him."

I know she's right, but I can't get my head around it. They were standing too close. Ms. Settles had her hand on Ryan's arm. They looked connected.

Jess asks, "Did you come today to spy on him? Or because you wanted to help? You don't even have world history with Settles."

"I—I wanted to be around Ryan," I confess. "And to help out, too. Helping the kids have fun is good."

"Then get your drink and let's go help. This is Lori's project, you know."

Great. So now Stiletto Settles has morphed into Lori in Jess's mind. I know when I'm outnumbered, so I bite my tongue and order my hot chocolate.

I've been working the fish pond a while and sipping my hot chocolate when Ryan returns. "Here's your drink," he says.

"Too late," I say, and waggle my cup at him. "I gave up on you and bought my own."

"Sorry," he says. "I got sidetracked."

"Really," I say, staring hard at him, but he just shrugs and sets down the paper cup he's been holding.

"In case you want another one."

I pick it up. "It's cold."

"I said I was sorry." He walks away to help two kids take fish off their magnets.

I remove the lid from the cold cup and pour the murky brown mixture on the ground, watching it soak into the grass without leaving a trace.

Ryan

"Seems like you're doing all right at school," Dad says.

We're driving home from McAllister's open house and our annual appearance in my classrooms for the meeting of parents and teachers. A stupid custom, especially in high school. I mean, who cares? In elementary school, parents are bumping into each other, the rooms are so crowded. By middle school, the crowds of "caring" parents have thinned, and by high school, most kids beg their families to stay away. Only nerds, geeks and superachievers have their parents hanging around. My dad's always gone, so going to these meetings is the dues he pays for all the travel that keeps him away from home. I'd rather he skipped it.

He looks over at me. "Your history teacher—what's her name?"

"Ms. Settles." My heart goes bump.

"She's a real looker. I'm telling you, teachers in my day were never that pretty."

"She's all right."

"Just all right? Then I'd like to see your idea of a pretty woman." He gives a short laugh.

He's making me mad. I don't like him talking about Lori this way. I don't like him thinking she's pretty.

"She had some nice things to say about you," Dad says.

"I like history more than I thought I would."

"Right." His voice drips with innuendo. "Anyway, I like her."

"She's old," I blurt out.

"Old? She's probably in her thirties. That's not old, son. Believe me."

"You want to date her?" I snap.

"Of course not. What's gotten into you, anyway?"

"Nothing." I slump down in the car, feeling like a pouting ten-year-old.

"Well, cut it out. I was just making conversation."

Dad doesn't date much these days, at least not when he's home. I have no idea what he does on the road. He could have another family for all I know. When I was in elementary school, he dated a few women. When I was in middle school, he hung with a woman named Diane, but they broke up after a year because he told her he didn't want to get married and didn't want her moving in. Cold. For a while, I missed her hanging around and cooking and all, but I got over it.

"You should start the college search, you know, looking into where you'd like to go, filling out some apps." Dad changes the subject.

"I got lots of time."

"No you don't. Aren't SATs coming up soon?"

"Took them already."

"Oh."

"You were in Michigan that weekend."

"I have to work. You know I'm here most weekends."

"I'm not complaining."

"How'd you do?"

I shrug. "Okay, I guess. The scores will be mailed. I can take them again next year, you know."

By now, we're home. As we go into the house, Dad says, "You seeing anyone?"

"What?"

"A girl. You have a girlfriend?"

"No. Why do you ask?"

He looks uncomfortable. "I'm not prying. Just wondering. Lots of good-looking girls at your school. When I was your age, I had a string of girlfriends."

Crap! I bite my tongue, hoping he doesn't start some dumb walk down memory lane. "Good for you." I start up the stairs to my room. "Got homework."

"We should talk more," he calls up after me.

Whatever, I think. "Sure," I say. In my room I push a pile of dirty clothes off my bed. The whole place is a mess, but I don't care. Unusual for me, because I like my stuff to be organized and neat. Lately I can't concentrate. It's as if some animal is prowling around inside my gut and wants out. I feel this gnawing sensation, as if my skin is on fire from the inside out. Joel says I need to get laid. That a guy can only do so much for himself in the shower alone. But the girls at school bore me. All except one.

I start piling up dirty laundry because if I don't wash soon, I'm out of shirts and jeans, and I can't go to school smelling like a locker room. I can't sit in front of Lori's desk reeking like a stupid jock. I toss the pile of dirties into a basket, promising myself I'll do it tomorrow after school, when I won't run into Dad downstairs. It's bugging me that he thinks Lori's hot. He's way too old to be lusting after her.

I turn on my computer and once it boots up, I go to my e-mail, where nine new messages are waiting for me. I haven't checked it since last night. Too busy when I got home today, what with the parent-teacher event tonight. I scroll down the list. Two from Honey. One from Joel. Some junk mail. One from "carnivaldaze." I almost delete it, then decide to open it. When the message flashes onto my screen, I about fall over. The time stamp is two a.m. the night before. It says:

Hello, Ry.

I hope you don't mind me e-mailing you. Sort of risky, I know. If you ever want to share another cappuccino, just to talk, let me know. Just hit reply and give me a time and date.

Please delete this after reading. L

I follow her instructions to the letter.

Lori

I can't sleep. It's three in the morning and my alarm will go off in only three hours and I can't get to sleep. I've cleaned my apartment—twice. Tried on clothes from my closet and made a pile to give away. I've surfed the Web, bought clothes and jewelry from a couple of sites, returned time and again to my e-mail program. I've watched TV, turned it off and on a dozen times. Infomercials are all that's on after one in the morning. Who buys this stuff?

Sometimes I feel like I want to crawl out of my skin. It itches. Burns. I take another bath. Nothing helps.

The parent-teacher meetings went well. No problems there. I return to the one with Ryan again and again. His blue eyes haunt me. His father came, not his mother. Usually it's the mother. Almost always, it's the mother, protector of her young, who shows up. Ryan is a softer version of his father, not yet gone to flab. The older man is beefy, with the pouchy jowl and paunchy midsection so common in middle-aged men. His hands are large and square and hairy, while Ryan's are young, long-fingered; the father's thumbnail, and only his thumbnail, is bitten to the quick. I think about the father touching me and my skin crawls. I think about Ryan touching me and I glow warm deep inside.

Bill Mathers, a coach at the school, divorced and the only bachelor, has asked me out. I almost laughed out loud. I see the way he looks at me, like some kind of wolf, ready to pounce and rip me open. Disgusting. They're all disgusting, these middle-aged men who think a woman owes them something. A date equals sex. Their math is so transparent.

My brain keeps coming back to Ryan, to his beauty, his youth. He's a puzzle to be put together. Behind the smart-aleck cracks in class, inside his easygoing exterior, there's a spring ready to uncoil. I must be careful. Careful as never before.

I return to my computer and scan the new arrivals in my inbox. Nothing I care about. I pace and drink red wine, hoping it will help me fall asleep. I slide a DVD into my machine and watch an old movie. At six, I shut off my alarm and begin to dress for school.

I look at my inbox one final time before heading out the door. A message has arrived marked with a red exclamation point. This one is urgent.

I read Ryan's reply, sent at 5:50 in the morning. He gives me the answer I want.

Ryan

On Friday night, I do exactly as Lori tells me. I wait at a certain bus stop, get into her car when she drives up and ride with her to another part of town, where we go into a coffee shop.

"It's my favorite coffeehouse," she says when we're inside, where it's dark and the walls are lined with booths for privacy.

Blue lights shine over the coffee bar, turning the place a shade like ocean water, deep and mysterious. A small band plays mellow jazz on a stage lit with revolving lights in pink, yellow and green. The smell of hot rich coffee makes the air chewy. We haven't talked much during the drive, and now that we're here my palms are sweating and my mouth is bone-dry. Lori takes a seat across from me in the booth, asks what I want when a waiter appears.

I stare at the menu with its two pages of coffee selections with names like Devil Mocha Delight, Vanilla

Extract, Double Whammy, Chili Pepper Surprise—
"brewed with hot peppers, and not for the taste timid,"
says the description. I can't concentrate.

"I like the Italian Stallion," Lori says, a smile in her
voice. "It's a dark-roasted Italian bean brewed with
licorice. Tasty."

"Sounds good," I say, hoping my voice doesn't
break, or squeak, or tremble. It holds steady.

She gives the waiter our coffee order, adding, "And
a slice of cinnamon coffee cake. Two forks."

I file the menu behind the sugar holder on the
wall, lock my fingers together on top of the table and
look across at her. For the first time tonight, our eyes
connect. She says, "I'm glad you came."

"Me too." My undeniable wit and charm, as
Honey jokes, escape me. How do I talk to this woman
who turns my insides to jelly and makes my blood
hot? Music? I can't believe she even listens to the tunes
I like. Sports? Cars? School? My mind's blank.

"You're awfully quiet. Anything wrong?"

"No. I—I'm just not sure—"

She covers my hands with hers. "I don't want to
make you uncomfortable, Ryan. I just want to get to
know you better. I want to enjoy your company. But
if you'd rather not—"

"No!" I blurt. "I—I mean, this is cool. I don't want
to leave or anything. I'm just digging around for
something to say."

"Words never fail you when you take me on in the classroom."

I see by her smile that she's teasing me, and I loosen up. "Well, then let's discuss world history— how about those Huns?" That makes her laugh and I feel a rush of relief. This might not be so hard after all.

"That's more like the Ryan I want to know."

The coffee comes, and the cake. I grab a fork and slice myself a chunk. "This is good."

Her smile widens. "Maybe I should have ordered two pieces."

I feel embarrassed and am glad the place is so dark. "I'll buy us another one."

"Don't be silly. I just want a taste." She slices off a sliver and eats it. I watch her red, red mouth the whole time.

She says, "I'm glad you and your father showed up at school the other night. So many parents blow off these meetings. I had five no-shows. Can you imagine? You're lucky to have a father interested enough in you to come."

"He tries," I say. "He travels a lot because of his work. I, um, hang by myself most weekdays." I don't know why I told her that. Why would she care?

"Yet you keep your grades up. That's commendable. Many teens left on their own would be less studious."

She sounds like a teacher and I feel something

cozy evaporate in the air between us. "Call me Mr. Studious."

"I couldn't help noticing your mother didn't come. Does she work nights?"

I stiffen. "She doesn't live with us."

"My parents are divorced too."

A natural assumption, but wrong. "They're not divorced. Mom's dead."

Lori's expression is shock, then sympathy. "I'm so sorry, Ryan. I had no idea."

"I don't talk about it."

"I can see this is painful for you—"

"Naw," I say, leaning back in the booth. "I don't remember her because it happened a long time ago—when I was two." Emotions come bubbling up in me and I push them down. "If Dad didn't have pictures, I wouldn't even know what she looked like."

She leans toward me, reaches for my hand, and I let her take hold. "Well, whoever raised you did a wonderful job. You are an intelligent and charming young man."

My insides go mushy. Lori's so beautiful, I just want to lean over and kiss her. Kiss her? What am I thinking?

"I used to want a mother more than anything. I asked Santa for one when I was four, but he didn't deliver." I give Lori a smile; Honey calls it my "now that you're hooked, let me reel you in" smile. I know whenever I'm doing it, and I turn it on high beam for Lori. "I'm over it now. A mother would only ask me a lot of questions like 'Where are you going?' and 'Who are you going with?' Who needs a surveillance junkie?" I'm thinking of Joel, whose mother plays Twenty Questions every time he starts to leave the house, and Honey's mother, who fires off a series of probes if she comes home fifteen minutes late.

"You may be right about mothers being over-rated," Lori says. "Some aren't worth much."

I wonder if she's referring to hers, but I don't ask. I'm totally into here and now. "Something I'll never know anything about," I say.

Lori sips her coffee. I watch her, feeling more comfortable by the minute. The gap between us has closed a little; I can almost forget that she's my teacher. We listen to the music together. "You have a better view of the quartet," she says. "Mind if I sit next to you so I can see them without turning around?"

I slide over and she joins me. When the outsides of our thighs touch, I feel a surge of energy shoot through me. Her perfume is all around me, and my jeans grow tighter in the crotch. She's staring straight ahead as if she doesn't even know the effect she's having on me. I swallow a mouthful of coffee and burn my tongue. The pain is the only thing that keeps my hands from touching her warm leg.

Once the set is over, Lori says, "We should leave before it gets any later."

I could sit here all night, but I agree. It's 10:45, and my curfew is 11:30, plus Dad's home from the road all this week.

In her car, Lori says, "I'll have to drop you at the end of your block. Is that all right?"

"Sure." The gap between us is widening again. I have no car. I have a curfew. I have a parent who'll ground me if I don't show up. I hate being such a kid!

When she stops at the top of my street, she says, "Here you are. Four houses down on the left. Sorry delivery can't be to your door, but I don't want anyone to see you get out of my car."

I nod, open the door. "I had a good time. Thanks." I settle on the word "good" because "mind-blowing" would be over the top.

"So did I."

I get out, wishing I didn't have to leave her.

She leans toward the passenger window as if she's forgotten to tell me something. "Maybe we can do it again sometime."

"Anytime." My mind grabs hold of the straw she's offering, and my gaze shifts to her breasts stretching her sweater tight. "Next time, I'll pay."

She laughs. "Absolutely."

I watch her drive away, shove my hands in my

pockets and head for my house. It's not until I'm up on the porch that it hits me—she never once asked me for directions to my home. She drove me straight here, knew just what house was mine, as if she's come here before.

Lori

The evening at the coffeehouse went better than I expected. Ryan was nervous. He's not shy; I know that from my classroom. But tonight I could see that he was uncomfortable and unsure of himself and of me. I did all I could to put him at ease and it worked. As I watched him loosen up and begin to talk, share and laugh, I was again struck at how mature he is for fifteen. And at how beautiful he is to me.

I was mature at fifteen too, but for different reasons. No matter now.

Being with Ryan makes me feel carefree and young. Tonight I wasn't the sexy Ms. Settles he knows from world history. I was Lori, the pretty girl in the back of one of my high school classrooms. I was the girl guys liked to look at and longed to touch. I want Ryan to touch me. I saw in his eyes that he wanted to. When our legs brushed against each other, I felt his muscles tense, saw his hand tighten around his coffee cup. Dead giveaways.

When he looked into my eyes, I knew what he was thinking, and even now, sitting here in the dark in my apartment, I relish the smoldering fire he's ignited in me. I can't wait to have his hands and mouth on my skin. I think about when it will happen, and where. I don't want to plan it. I want it to happen when he's as ready in his head as he is in his body. And it *will* happen. I know it just as surely as I stare out at the night sky.

I take a sip from my wineglass, roll the stem between my fingers. The information about his mother was surprising. He wouldn't tell me how she died, and I knew better than to press him about it. He'll tell me when he's ready. Until then, I'll be patient and understanding. So very understanding.

Our coming together is like a slow dance to be savored and enjoyed. We come close, touch, retreat, spin and balance with purposeful and intricate steps that will lead to only one place. My anticipation is all-consuming.

Ryan

Lori and I go to the coffeehouse a lot. Mostly on weeknights when my dad's out of town. She picks me up after dark at the end of my block after we make sure no one's watching. I like being with her. I like talking to her. It's hard in the beginning, but then not at all. She tells me that she grew up in Seattle, went to college in California.

She says, "I always knew I'd be a teacher. When I was a little girl, I'd play school in my room by lining up all my dolls and stuffed animals and teaching them their ABCs."

"Did they learn them?" I ask.

This makes her laugh. "Only in my imagination. I was an amazing teacher in my imagination, and could make a teddy bear do anything."

"Do you have sisters? Brothers?"

"I'm an only child."

"Me too."

"Did you want siblings?" she asks.

I shrug. "Not really. Growing up, Dad never stuck with one woman long enough for me to think about it. He dated a few women with kids, but I never really liked any of them—the kids, I mean. They were always messing with my stuff and I didn't like that. I'm not a slob," I say. "I sort of like things neat and organized."

"It doesn't surprise me. I see it in your handwriting in the work you turn in."

"You do?"

She pats my arm. "Don't panic. It's a good thing. I took some handwriting-analysis courses in college. It's been helpful to me in my classrooms."

"But what do you see in me?"

"I see that you're smart and sensitive and older than your years."

I like hearing this part. I want her to think of me as mature, not some dumb kid hanging on her every word. "Dad's pressuring me to start looking at colleges. I've been thinking about it. Where I want to go. Out of state or not."

"I paid my own way through college," she volunteers.

"Were you poor?"

"No. But I didn't want anything from my father."

Her mouth is in a hard line whenever she mentions her parents.

"I like my dad well enough," I say.

"He's a good father. Mine wasn't."

"Your mother?"

"Not a very good one either."

I want to know more, but start to think I shouldn't be prying. I don't want her to tune me out, drop me. At some point, when we talk, we start holding hands. I like the way it feels. I like the way she makes me feel. It's hard for me not to tell her that. Harder and harder for me to keep from touching her. I like watching her face when we talk, and the way her body sways when a jazz group plays music, and the sound of her voice tickling my ear when she leans over to whisper to me. It takes all my willpower to get out of her car after being with her all evening. To go home alone and go to bed with my head all around her and my body on fire.

I've taken so many cold showers that my skin's started to wrinkle and my balls have shriveled. I wash my sheets a lot because of Lori. There's no way I can wash my mind of her.

Honey

I open our front door when the bell rings unexpectedly and stare out at Ryan. He's grinning like a fool, as if popping over on a Saturday morning were a regular habit instead of a sometime thing. As if we're friends again instead of strangers. "Selling magazine subscriptions?" I ask. Sure, my heart's in my throat because he's shown up without warning, but I'm mad at him because he's been too "busy" to hang with me for over a month.

"It's freezing out here. Can I come in?"

"Knock yourself out." I walk away and he follows.

"Hey, what's your problem?"

I head down to our walk-out basement, which my parents let me take over when friends come, before I say a word to him. "You haven't been around very much," I tell him.

"I'm here now."

I'd love to lay into him, but I don't want him to leave, either. "What's the occasion?"

"Just thought I'd say hi. When did I ever need a reason?"

"I guess you don't," I say, backing down from a fight. Just seeing him makes my knees weak. "Joel and Jess are coming over. Joel has a DVD copy of some concert for us to watch. And Jess made brownies. Want to stay?"

He shoves his hands into the pockets of his jeans and rocks back and forth in his boots. "Am I welcome?"

Before I can answer, my kid brother comes barreling down the stairs. His face lights up when he sees Ryan, and Ryan waves. Cory comes over, impulsively hugs Ryan. No one can ever predict how Cory is going to act, and today he's excited to see Ryan. I envy his escape into Ryan's arms. By the time Joel and Jess arrive, Cory and Ryan are tossing a ball to each other.

"Hey, man." Joel looks surprised to see Ryan. "Didn't know you were going to be here."

"He just showed," I explain.

Jess gives me an "are you keeping secrets from me?" look and I shake my head. No way.

"Can't I hang with old friends without them freaking?" Ryan asks. He's sounding irritated.

"It's just been a while," Joel says. "Where have you been? What's been going on?"

I'm glad he's asking and not me.

"Well, I'm here now. How about that DVD? Is it worth watching?"

Distraction. Split the offense. Answer a question with another question. I've seen Ryan use the technique before.

Joel reaches inside his jacket and pulls out a shiny disk. "Bootleg copy, so the quality isn't great, but it's still good."

I send Cory upstairs and he goes without a peep, and we all snuggle into the beat-up sofa and watch the DVD. I'm next to Ryan and his body heat makes it hard to concentrate on the grainy video. He smells good too, like cinnamon and warm sugar and sandalwood. A man-made male scent that smells grown-up and sophisticated.

When the DVD is over, we talk about the group and their music, then about school. It's Joel who says, "So have you heard if Lori Settles has said yes to Coach Mathers yet?"

"Yes to what?" Ryan is twirling a small cushion between his hands. He stops cold.

"Where have you been? It's all over the locker room. Old Mathers has been asking her out. The poor horny guy."

"She should go," Jess says.

"Why should she?" Ryan asks. He's sitting straighter and his eyes look wary, but no one has noticed except me, because I notice everything about Ryan.

"To give the old guy a thrill?" Joel says. "He really has the hots for her. Don't you notice the way he looks at her?"

"He gets all red in the face if she just walks past," I say. Mathers is the girls' basketball coach. I like the man, but he's under Ms. Settles' spell totally. "He all but drools if they're in the cafeteria together."

Jess sighs and flops backward. "Is she all you guys talk about in the locker room?"

Joel covers Jess's ears and winks. "I can't say what we talk about where she's involved. Too crude for your sweet ears."

Ryan stands. "Listen, I got some things to do before Dad gets home."

"I thought he was off the road."

"He got held over in Chicago. He'll be back tomorrow afternoon."

I follow Ryan up the stairs, wishing he would stay. "You want to come over for dinner? I know Mom and Dad would like to see you. And Mom never minds when you eat with us. It's been a long time."

At the front door, Ryan turns. "Rain check."

He blesses me with a melting smile. "See you in school."

I watch him hurry away, and wish with all my heart that I didn't love him so much. And that for once, just once, he'd look at me the way Coach Mathers looks at Lori Settles.

Ryan

"Are you dating Coach? How many times have you gone out with him?" We're sitting in Lori's car, in the rain, in front of her apartment. As soon as I left Honey's, I called her, said I had to see her, took a bus to her neighborhood and walked the rest of the way, meeting her at her car. We were supposed to go to "our" coffeehouse tonight, but I can't think of anything except Lori and Coach. I see pictures of them inside my mind, of him doing with her what I want to do with her.

"Mathers? I don't know. Who keeps count?"

"So you are dating him?"

She turns in the driver's seat to face me. "Is this an interrogation? I don't have to account for the things I do with my time."

My stomach feels as if I've swallowed a hard cold stone. "I—I thought . . . I was special. That we were special."

Her expression softens. "We are. Very special."

Rain is pelting the windows, sluicing in long noisy rivers along the glass, like a knife cutting through my heart. The windows are fogged, moist from our breath and the heat of my anger. Hot wetness swells behind my eyes. I'm acting like a jerk, but I can't help myself. I have to know the truth about her and Coach.

"Ryan." Lori reaches over, places her palm on my cheek, rubs her thumb across my skin. "Are you jealous?"

I can hardly breathe. Every cell in my body is screaming and on fire. "Of course I am," I say. The confession hurts like crazy on its way out of my mouth.

"Oh, my dear, precious Ryan." She leans forward, lifts my face and kisses me lightly on the mouth.

I take her shoulders and kiss her back. Hard, I kiss her, and long. Her tongue slides between my teeth, igniting a fever I can't control. Outside, the rain drums on the glass, giving a rhythm to some primitive force in me that I don't want to control.

Her hand slips onto my crotch, cups the bulge pushing against my jeans and makes me groan. She rubs me and I think I'm going to burst. "Do you like that?" she asks.

"Yes." I kiss her again, driving my tongue into her wet, hot mouth.

We're both breathing heavily and all I want is her

body against mine. I struggle to get closer, but the gearshift pokes me in the stomach. I break our kiss long enough to gasp from the pain.

Her eyes are wide, her pupils large, staring holes in my face. "What do you want?" she asks, her voice low and whispery. "Tell me what you want."

"You," I say.

She opens the door and the car fills with cold wet air. The rain plasters her sweater to her body, showing me every curve in detail. I see the shape of her bra and her breasts. I want to touch her so much it hurts. "Come upstairs," she says.

I go, not feeling the rain, only the heat from inside my body. She opens the door and for a minute we stand on the rug inside it, dripping wet, shivering. And then her mouth is on mine and her hands are tugging at my jeans. Somehow, I don't remember how, we're in her bedroom and our clothes have come off. We're in her soft bed, and just before I think I'm going to explode, she hands me a foil packet from her bedside table and says, "Put this on."

My hands are shaking so hard I can't open the wrapper, so she helps. And then the world goes away and there's Lori, only Lori, filling my universe.

PART
2

Lori

I watch Ryan sleep. The rise and fall of his chest is mesmerizing. The light from the lamp makes his skin glisten. His body is beautiful. I knew it would be. The long muscles of his arms and legs look loose and limber, no longer coiled with energy. His face is serene, no longer brimming with passion and need. I like that look that says hunger on his face. The one that says, "I want you."

We've been on this collision course for months. From the first time I saw him in my classroom, I knew that, with planning, we'd be at this place where we are tonight. Ryan with me, in my bed. Tonight, he wanted me, needed me. And I need him, too. He won't believe that if I tell him. He could never know how satisfying it is to have him touch me, his young hands stroking my skin. I rise inside like a surfer cresting on a wave, hovering in the curl, hiding in the blue-green water until the last moment before it breaks and sends me to shore.

Now Ryan sleeps. When he wakes, we'll have to talk about what has happened. I'll console him if he's sorry, which I don't think he will be. Males rarely are.

Ryan

I wake up and I'm confused, disoriented. I see a room bathed in lamplight, but it's not my room. I sit up and see Lori sitting in a chair by the window. She's staring at me. I'm naked and feel embarrassed. "You okay?" I ask.

"Are you?"

I hear a catch in her voice, so I grab the comforter and wrap it around myself, cross the room and kneel beside the chair. I can see she's been crying. "What's wrong?" Instantly I think I've disappointed her, that I didn't do something right.

"Are you sorry?" she asks.

"Are you?"

She smooths my hair. "I will never be sorry."

Relief floods through me. "Me neither."

"I—I've wanted to kiss you for a long time."

"Me too. I mean, I've wanted to kiss you, too." My head's spinning because we've done a lot more than kiss. Our first time together at the coffeehouse comes back to me, how insecure and inadequate I felt. I don't want to feel inadequate now. I want to feel the power I felt when we were in bed, Lori moving and moaning. I don't know what to say.

"Did I make you happy?" she asks.

"Happy?" I don't exactly know what she means.

"Like other girls you've been with."

"T-there haven't been others," I say, but I turn away from her.

"It isn't necessary to lie, Ryan. I can handle the truth."

"All right." I tell my story, getting out as much as I can as fast as I can, hoping I don't turn Lori off. "The truth is that I've been close to doing this with a few girls, but that was mostly in middle school when we were playing kissing games and drinking. Once I was shut in a closet with some girl and we heard all our friends telling us to get it on and I wanted to, but she started crying and saying she didn't want to do it for the first time in a closet with a guy who was basically a stranger. So we lied to the others when we came out. I never did anything like that again. I decided to save the sex until I cared about a girl."

She stares at me for a long time before saying, "Then I'm glad I can be your first."

"Me too. I'm glad about you wanting to be with me."

She lowers her head, and her hair falls like a veil around her face. "You don't think badly of me, do you?"

"No way! You're beautiful and I wanted this to happen more than anything."

She looks up. "Are you sure?"

"And . . . and I want it to happen again."

She's been holding her hands in her lap, but now she reaches out and cups my face. "We'll have to be very careful. If anyone finds out—"

"Do I look stupid? Do you think I'll blab this all over school?"

"I hope not."

My heart is thudding. How can I convince her? "I won't."

She lets out her breath as if she's been holding it for a long time. "Then we'll have to set up a system so that no one will ever suspect."

"You're carnivaldaze," I say, because that's how we've gotten messages to each other about meeting at the coffeehouse. "She can e-mail me anytime. No one will ever know."

Lori smiles, leans forward and kisses me lightly. "Well, right now I'd better drive you home before you miss your curfew."

I sway forward on my knees, catch her hands in mine. "Dad's stuck in Chicago. He won't be in until really late."

She studies me. "Truth?"

"I wouldn't lie."

She stands and so do I. She hugs me and I feel my heart race. "Then no use rushing off, is there? Come back to bed with me."

She doesn't have to ask me twice.

Honey

Something's up with Ryan. I don't know what, but something is making him different these days. When I say this to Jess, she rolls her eyes and says, "Why do you think that? He's been doing his own thing since school started. How can he be even more different?"

"I'm a dedicated Ryan watcher. I know when changes are made."

Jess is so into Joel she wouldn't notice if the sun set in the east. We're on our way to go Christmas shopping in one of Atlanta's trendy boutique areas. Taylor's driving, and now she chimes in with "You need to get over him, girlfriend."

"I am over him."

"Sure you are," my friends say in unison.

"In a romantic way," I clarify. "I still care about him as a friend."

"So what changes have you noticed?" Taylor asks.

I know she's humoring me, but still I speak up. "He hardly ever returns my IMs or e-mails. It's like he's never home. No more text messages, either. I have to practically trip him in the halls to get him to speak. It's like his head's in another universe."

"Joel says they don't hang much anymore either," Jess offers.

"How can they?" Taylor says. "You two are joined at the hip."

"We haven't joined anything yet," Jess says. "You know I'd spill my guts to my best friends if our body parts 'joined.' "

Taylor and I laugh. Jess points, saying, "Parking space alert! That SUV is pulling out. Grab the spot."

We wait patiently for the Mom-mobile to back out of its diagonal space. Just as we're leaving the car, Taylor says, "Oh, oh! I have dirt." We wait for her to divulge. "The admin crowd is asking Settles to back down on the sexy clothing."

"That's going to break some male hearts," Jess remarks.

I ask, "Who says?"

"My mom." Taylor's mother is a PTO heavyweight and has her fingers in all things McAllister High.

"I like Ms. Settles," Jess says. "She's nice and cracks jokes in class. Cuts us some slack on assignments, too."

"Well, the principal told her to tone down the outfits."

"They're all jealous because she's pretty and wears heels," Jess says. "That's a totally athletic-shoe crowd in the front office."

I don't say anything because I don't like Lori Settles. There's something too nice about her. That, and Ryan thinks she's hot.

"It's the stilettos," Taylor says. "Who can walk in them?"

We've been walking and talking, but suddenly Jess stops. "Let's try some on."

We're in front of a high-end shoe boutique. "We can't afford anything in there."

"We're not buying," Taylor says. "Just shopping."

We giggle our way inside, where a saleswoman looks us over, then asks, "May I help you?"

"I want to try on those," Taylor says, pointing to a pair of black sky-high Pradas. "Size seven."

The woman's gaze flicks over Taylor's sweater and jeans. It's obvious we're not Atlanta belles, but still she disappears into a back room, emerging minutes later with a box.

"I want to try these," Jess says, holding up an equally high-heeled shoe. "Size six and a half."

The woman looks at me. "And you?"

My face gets hot, but I grab a strappy evening shoe and hold it toward her. "Size ten." She stares at me. "Basketball," I say boldly. "It makes a girl's feet bigger."

We laugh together the minute she's gone. When she returns, we try on our selections and Taylor takes a few wobbly steps. "It takes practice," the saleswoman says, watching us from the ankles down, and for a second I think she's going to throw her body over the shoes to protect them from us.

I feel very unsteady, but brave a brief walk to a floor mirror to admire the sparkly crystal-studded shoes and how elegant they make my feet look. I totally get why Lori Settles wears them. They do a lot for a girl's morale.

Once we leave the store, we can't stop laughing. "I have new respect for models," Taylor says.

"And for Ms. Settles," Jess adds. "How does she do it?"

We're still laughing when we pass a street vendor with a table full of handmade silver jewelry. "Earring alert," Taylor says.

"All handmade by me," a hippie-looking girl tells us.

"Nice," I say, my eye drawn to a necklace. A loop of silver twisted into a knot dangles from the chain.

"It's a Celtic lovers' knot," the girl tells me. "Very meaningful for lovers. No one else sells them in Atlanta."

"Then I'll have to buy these," I say, picking up a pair of silver dangle earrings with a chip of turquoise. "For my mom. I love her, but . . ."

The girl laughs and wraps my purchase.

My friends and I shop for a few more hours, then head home. I hide my purchases in a hatbox on my closet shelf, go to my computer and punch up my e-mail program. My heart's beating faster, high on hope that Ryan's sent me an e-card for Thanksgiving because I sent him one—a funny one, naturally. But except for junk mail and a reminder from Coach Mathers about basketball practice starting up on Monday, I have no other messages. I feel let down. Stupid, I tell myself. He doesn't even remember I'm alive.

Ryan

I walk on air for weeks. What happened—what is happening—between me and Lori is like something in a movie, or a dream. My biggest problem is controlling myself. I want to be with her all the time. I want to touch and taste her, have more sex with her. It's all I think about. In the classroom, she treats me the way she does every other student. She never looks me in the eye, though. Too dangerous. As if our feelings will burst out like water from a dam. So I slouch in my chair, put in my time, cut out as soon as I can, go home and stay in my room, sending her explicit e-mails and arranging times to get together.

I never appreciated my dad's work schedule so much. He's gone, and the housekeeper hardly notices me, so I come and go as I please. I usually catch a city bus to Lori's neighborhood and walk to her apartment complex. I forward the home phone to my cell so I'm always available if Dad calls from the road. Lori often serves takeout when I come over, but we don't waste much time eating.

At some point, she tells me, "For the record, I've never gone out with Mathers."

I wonder why I ever got so worked up about that. "It's a free world," I say. We're on her sofa, half watching a DVD.

"Are you dating anyone?"

"How can you ask me that?"

"It's a logical question. I know you have a life outside of us."

No, I don't, I think. "You and school," I say.

"What about your friends?"

"What about them?"

"You don't mind spending so much time with me? Don't they ask questions?"

"Only Honey Fowler. You remember her."

"The girl who likes you."

I scoff. "We're just friends. For years."

Lori gives me a skeptical look. "Well, she isn't that pretty. Not your type."

"What is my type?"

Lori leans over and kisses my neck, sending shivers up my body. "I am."

"Prove it."

She does.

• • •

"What do you want to do over Christmas break?" my dad asks me when I walk into the kitchen on a Saturday morning in December.

Spend every second with Lori, I think. "I don't know . . . hang, I guess." I go to the fridge and pull out the OJ.

"Come on, you must want to do something fun. I'm off the road until after New Year's."

The realization hits me—Dad's going to be home 24/7 for two full weeks. I take a swig from the carton, set it on the countertop. "What do you want to do?"

"Road trip?"

"I'm too old for Disney World."

"We could buzz up to Baltimore and see your aunt Debbie. She's invited us."

She's Dad's sister and lives up there with her husband and my two boring cousins, Robbie and Karen. "Whoopee," I say.

"I don't like your attitude."

"You want me to be honest, don't you?"

"I want you to act as if you care about something—anything. You disappear into your room when I'm home. God knows what you do when I'm not."

I hold my breath, exhale slowly. No good will come of pissing him off. Especially when I want a car for Christmas. Man, if I had a car, I could hook up with Lori more often. Riding the bus is really getting to be a drag. She takes me home after dark, some- times will even pick me up, but not too often, just in case anyone's watching. If someone finds out . . .

"Going to Baltimore will be fine," I say.

Dad looks surprised. I guess he didn't expect me to cave without more arguing. "Well then, okay. I'll call Debbie and tell her to expect us for Christmas. We can go into D.C. and see the Capitol, the White House, and the Smithsonian—that's one great museum."

He's getting excited just talking about it, while I'm getting sick just thinking about it. What fun . . . a road trip to Washington to look at boring buildings and visit relatives I don't even like. I turn and fish two pieces of bread from the cupboard and plop them into the toaster, but my appetite's totally gone.

Lori

Being with Ryan feeds something deep inside me I can't describe. Such a beautiful boy. And so willing and eager to make me happy. His enthusiasm is an elixir. Even the way he avoids eye contact with me in the classroom is exciting. This thing between us is like water simmering on a low, constant fire. I need him. He makes me feel alive. Especially now.

I was called into the main office for a conference with the powers that be. It seems my "apparel" is offending some of the faculty and some of my students' parents. It makes my blood boil. The old hags. I look at the way they dress, like bag ladies. They hate my high heels most of all. Why shouldn't they? Lumbering around like water buffaloes in their sensible shoes. Our esteemed principal, Estelle Dexter, kept coming back to my heels time and again. She cited "insurance concerns" as the reason I need to lose them in the classroom when I teach.

"What if you fall? These floors can be really slick. If you fall, you'll hurt yourself, maybe even break a leg or something. That will keep you from doing your job. It won't help lower insurance rates, either," Dexter tells me.

"Fall? I don't think that's a problem for me. I'm very physically fit."

"Yes, everyone can see that you're fit." Her tone is condescending. She taps a pencil on the edge of her desk. "Ms. Settles—Lori—please don't make this an issue. Your attire just isn't absolutely appropriate for the classroom. There are impressionable young people, immature young men. No sense inflaming them."

Inflaming them! How dare she say this to me? "Have my students complained about my teaching methods? My lack of skill in imparting world history to them?"

"No, not at all, but that's not the issue. I don't understand why you're getting so worked up about this. It's a simple request."

"It speaks to my character. As if a woman in a dress and heels is somehow unfit to stand in front of a class-room."

Her mouth puckers and tightens. "I regret you see things that way. However, this isn't up for debate. Change your way of dressing. Don't make me draw the county superintendent into this."

My blood's boiling and I want to reach across her

desk and choke her. The sanctimonious old bitch. I could make a case to the teachers' union, fight for my rights. Then I think of how ugly such a case could get. Sides would be taken. Kids would be jacked around. I'd lose my ability to see Ryan every day. I stifle my fury and ask, "And just what do you consider acceptable attire?"

She looks mollified and comes in for the kill. "Longer skirts, more coverage of your cleavage, heels no more than two inches high, nothing too avant-garde."

In other words, look like a frump. I stand. "Are we through?"

"Yes. Have a good day."

I walk out of the office and go into the faculty lounge, so angry I can hardly speak. Only Mr. Ishiwata, the music instructor, is there, on break. He looks up, smiles, but his smile quickly fades. "Is something wrong, Ms. Settles?"

Only if you count being told by your principal that you look like a whore. "Nothing a cup of coffee won't cure," I say as pleasantly as I can. I know Mr. Ishiwata isn't one of my enemies. I've seen the way he looks at my breasts—his favorite part of a woman's body, I'm betting.

"Please, let me pour you a cup."

He's solicitous and too eager, but that always

works to my advantage. "That would be kind," I say. "Two sweeteners and some cream."

He falls over himself fixing the coffee, brings it to me ceremoniously and sets it on the table in front of me. "Thank you," I say.

His eyes are magnified behind his glasses. I turn, lean slightly forward and give him a full look down the front of my dress at the curve of my breasts pushing up from my lacy black bra. He blinks and stares hard. I lean back and sip the coffee.

"It is my pleasure," he says, and leaves the lounge.

I think, Lecher. All men are lechers, but I know how to handle them. Just the way I know I'll handle Dexter's unreasonable request. I want to stay under her radar, and causing a scene over my clothes won't accomplish that. I calm myself with thoughts of Ryan, of his smooth young body, of his raw and hungry passion.

Everything else is a distraction.

Ryan

I know the location of purgatory—my aunt's house in Baltimore. Dad and I arrive four days before Christmas. By day two I want to go home. My cousins make me nuts. Especially Karen, all of twelve and hanging on me all the time with her silly girlfriends.

"Where's your mom?" one of them asks. "Why didn't she come with you?"

Karen elbows the nosey girl in the ribs. "Shhh. I told you, he doesn't have a mother."

The girl turns beet red and I grit my teeth but smile at her anyway. "No mom to nag me," I say.

"Lucky," the girl says.

All I think about is getting back to Lori. She wasn't very happy when I told her I was leaving, the night before Dad and I flew out. "But what about our Christmas?" she said. "I bought you presents." Her apartment was decorated and there were fresh logs in the fireplace.

"We'll just have to wait until I get home."

"You should have told me sooner. Why didn't you say something before now? We e-mail every day."

"No freedom of movement when my dad's in town, and I didn't want to tell you in an e-mail. But as soon as school starts again, he'll be heading to the Midwest for a five-day medical sales convention. I can stay over. I saved it as a surprise." Lori has been asking me to spend a whole night with her, and now I can.

That made her smile. "Maybe I'll forgive you."

I sneak her an e-mail from my aunt's. I'm so bored and craving contact with my real life that I e-mail Honey, too. Lori doesn't e-mail me back, but Honey does. She writes a long story about Cory and their Christmas turkey that makes me laugh out loud. I've forgotten how funny she can be. I realize that I miss her and promise myself that once I'm home, I'll reestablish contact.

Dad takes me and the cousins into D.C., where we visit every historical landmark in the city. Or it feels as if we do. Honey sends me a text message to say hello to the president, and I text back that if I can get past the Secret Service and into the Oval Office, I will. Keeping in touch with Honey helps me feel grounded. The girl's a real lifeline.

When we're in the Smithsonian gift shop, I remember that I don't have a Christmas gift for Lori, so I poke around and finally settle on a necklace from one of their ancient-history collections. A good move, I figure, because she's into history and it's real silver but doesn't cost a bundle.

Two other things happen while we're in Baltimore—I don't get a car for Christmas, and I turn sixteen. Aunt Debbie bakes a cake and everyone sings and Dad keeps saying how important family is and I try to act as if I care. By the time we fly home, I'm about ready to jump out of my skin. The first person I contact is Lori.

She asks, "When can I see you?"

"Two days. Dad's leaving on Tuesday."

"I don't want to wait that long."

This makes me feel really good, but tonight Honey, Joel, Jess and a few more of my friends are coming over. I've been looking forward to seeing everyone again. I want Lori bad, but I know we'll have more time if we wait a few days. "I can't help it," I tell her. "I'll see you in class tomorrow." The holidays are over and it's back to the salt mines.

There's a long pause on my cell, so long that I wonder if she's still on the line. "Lori?"

"I'm here. Just disappointed. I thought you'd want me."

"I want you like crazy. I have a hard-on just hearing your voice." She says some things that make me hot and I almost fold. "Two days," I say. "It'll be even better because we have to wait. Anticipation can be a good thing."

She hangs up and a jolt of fear goes through me. What if she blows me off? Being with Lori is the best thing that's ever happened to me.

Before I can decide what to do, Joel shows up with Jess. Honey arrives and so do Taylor, Peter, Kevin and his girl. It's good to see them all, talk to them and hang out, so I shove Lori to the back of my mind. We head downstairs to my rec room to listen to tunes and dance.

Honey

Hanging out with Ryan and all our friends is the best part of my holidays. I love being with everyone; it's like old times, before we all started high school and drifted apart. I linger after the others leave. Mom's going to yell because it's late and tomorrow school starts up again, but I don't care. Being with Ryan again, even as a friend, is worth any grief I get from my mother.

"Let me see what you brought home from D.C.," I say when we're alone.

"In my room."

We go upstairs. His room is neat as a pin. Same old Ryan. "My room looks like a campground for the homeless," I say. "How do you do this? More to the point, why do you do it?"

"Habit. I hate messes," he says, pulling out his desk chair for me. He hands me a clear container full of brochures. "My Christmas vacation in a box."

I sort through the pile. "Is there any place you didn't go?"

"I didn't make it to the Oval Office," he says with a grin. "Don't tell Dad, but the Smithsonian was pretty cool. You should have seen the aviation room and the gems rooms. One diamond was this big." He holds his thumb and forefinger apart.

Just then, his cell rings. He glances at the display, looks at me, then down at the ringing phone. "I have to take this. Old friend." I could swear he's nervous.

"Should I leave?"

"No . . . I'll take it in the hall. Stay put."

I sit alone, wondering why he's acting flustered. I don't care who calls him. . . . Okay, maybe I care just a little. But it's odd. We've just spent an evening with all our friends. I sigh, set the container on the floor and cruise the room. I feel good being with him. He's more like the old Ryan, my friend from years past.

As I pass his dresser, I see a small black velvet box, the kind that usually holds jewelry. Back off, Honey, I tell myself. But I don't. I grab the box and open it. Inside is a necklace, a chain of hammered silver with a twist of curved silver strands dangling from the center. Where have I seen this before? Somewhere . . . Inside the lid is printed SMITHSONIAN GIFT SHOP in old-English-looking type.

Then it hits me. This is one of those Celtic love knots like the girl on the street was selling on the day

Jess, Taylor and I went shopping. But why did Ryan buy something like this in Washington as a souvenir? A sick feeling hits my stomach—the slap of rejection mingles with the burn of jealousy. Does he have a girl-friend? One he's never told me about? I rack my brain, trying to imagine who it is. I come up blank.

I hear him heading down the hall. I snap the lid shut and drop the box where I found it. I'm back in the chair when he returns.

"Sorry," he says, coming into the room.

"No problem," I say, knowing it's a lie. I have a problem. A big problem. I want to know, what's going on in Ryan's life?

Ryan

When I enter Lori's classroom on the first day back, I'm shocked. She's dressed like a character from *Little House on the Prairie*—a white blouse buttoned to her neck, a skirt to the floor and weird-looking old-lady shoes. She's still pretty, though.

One of the girls asks, "What's up, Ms. Settles?"

"Canada, Alaska, the North Pole," Lori says, making everyone laugh. "Do you mean my new wardrobe?"

"Yeah," another girl says.

"Glad you noticed."

I'm staring but keeping my mouth shut.

"Request from the front office," Lori says.

Kids groan. "Can they do that? Make you change the way you dress?" someone asks.

"They can send any of you home if you arrive dressed against their rules, can't they?"

A grumble races through the room. "But you're a teacher. You're a grown-up."

"If they can do it to you, they can do it to me," she says.

"It sucks!" yells some guy in the back.

"Rules are rules," Lori says. She's vented to me in private, so I know how she feels about the administration and Mrs. Dexter—"the old hag"—and how much she's hating this. It must be hard for her to act as if she doesn't really care. "Now, let's get to work."

I think about the rules we're breaking, she and I. What would the principal say if she knew what Lori and I were doing right under her nose?

Once class is over and I'm going out the door, Lori says, "Ryan, can I see you a minute? About that special assignment I gave you?"

Two people waiting to walk with me look curious. I wave them on and go to Lori's desk. My heart is thumping like a drum. For safety's sake, she always steers clear of talking to me after class.

Her eyes laser into me. "Is your special assignment on target?"

Code for "Is your dad out of the house?"

"On target," I say. The room is empty and we're alone.

"I'll pick you up at the bus stop. The one near your house."

"I can ride."

"I don't want to wait," she says. Her voice is tight and sharp.

"All right."

"And bring your things," she says. "For the night."

There's a bitchy bossiness about her that turns me off, but I nod anyway. And when I think about spending a whole night with her, I breathe hard.

Our clothes come off the minute we walk into her place, and our sex is wild and fast. When it's over, Lori dresses in a silky robe. She pops the cork of a bottle of champagne and pours two glasses. I've never drunk champagne but don't want to tell her that. I'm a beer guy. Joel and I got into my dad's bourbon once when we were in seventh grade. I felt great, all spaced out and soaring, until I got sick and tossed it all on the bathroom floor. Dad was better about it than I thought he'd be. He said, "A rite of passage, but don't do it again until you're legal." I got grounded for two weeks, and a lock went on the cabinet, but he didn't go postal the way Joel's mother did when she found out.

"I've saved these for you," Lori says, handing me a stack of presents.

I'm surprised because there are so many boxes. "I—I only got you one thing."

"That's not what it's about. I want you to have nice things. I want to show you how much I care."

I open boxes of cool shirts, a leather Harley vest, CDs by the hottest artists on the charts and, finally, an iPod. "Wow," I tell her. "I've been wanting one of these. Thanks."

"I'm glad you like it."

I'm blown away but try not to show it. I retrieve my backpack and pull out the black velvet box. "Sorry it's not wrapped." I feel like a miser, offering her one tiny present.

"Not to worry." She opens the box and I see her eyes light up. "A Celtic love knot! I love it."

"You know what it is? I didn't. I had to read about it." Relief goes through me.

"Put it on me." She hands me the necklace, turns and lifts her dark hair, showing me the soft tight white skin of her neck. The sight arouses me. I ease on the necklace, and she turns back toward me. Her hand slides down my body and I shiver. Her mouth ignites me. She slips off her robe and pulls me on top of her, wearing only my necklace until we're finished.

Ryan

I've always slept by myself, never shared mattress space with anyone. I sleep hard at first, but when I wake up, the room is dark and I don't know where I am. I panic. Then I remember. I'm at Lori's. I drank too much, but not enough to get sick. Already learned that lesson.

I touch the place beside me in the bed, but Lori isn't there. I hear a noise from outside the bedroom, find my jeans on the floor and tug them on. I come out into a brightly lit room and squint, a headache exploding my brain. "Lori?"

"In here," she answers.

I go to the kitchen and she's down cleaning the floor with a sponge. Weird!

"What are you doing?" I look at the stove's digital clock and read 3:00 a.m. "Did you spill something?"

She stands up. "No. I have trouble sleeping."

"So you're cleaning?" Weirder!

She drops the sponge in the sink and comes to me, loops her arms around me. "A lifelong problem. Don't think about it. When I wake up and can't go back to sleep, I just get up instead of lying in the dark. Tonight, I decided to clean. See? No damage from our party for two."

The place is spotless. "I would have helped."

"You were sound asleep." She nuzzles my neck. "You're pretty cute when you're asleep."

I hear that tone in her voice that says, "Let's get it on," but right now, my head hurts and I'm not in the mood for another round of burning up her sheets. "Let's just go get some sleep," I say.

She pulls back, a pout on her mouth. Under the overhead light, I notice the lines around her colorless lips and at the corners of her eyes. The last girl I was this close to was Janey Smythe, at an eighth-grade dance. She didn't have any lines on her face, just clear smooth skin, luscious enough to lick. Fortunately I didn't.

I back away from Lori, yawn and stretch. "I'll be in the bedroom." I say it in a way that doesn't offer her an invitation. All I want is to go to bed and get some sleep.

"I'll be in later," she says, her voice cool.

"Whatever," I say, and leave her standing alone in the kitchen.

• • •

"You look rough," Dad tells me a few nights later over dinner.

"Been staying up late, studying," I mumble. In truth, I hustled home this afternoon after three nights at Lori's, threw in a load of wash and made the place look as if I'd been living here.

"Those teachers shouldn't work you so hard."

No work involved, I think. "You warned me that high school wasn't a cakewalk." In dealing with parents, it's a good idea to feed them back the lines they've used on you.

"That's true, especially if a student has his sights on college."

"Like I do," I say. I haven't thought about college or homework or anything except Lori for months. The only reason I'm keeping up is because she helps me with my assignments. I almost blew a test before Christmas, but my other work was good enough to help me skate by.

"Where'd you get the iPod and new clothes?"

Dad's question comes out of left field. Adrenaline pumps, turning my brain to mush. "What?"

"I saw the stuff stacked on your bed. Just wondering where it came from."

Stupid! In my hurry to get other things done, I left Lori's gifts lying out in the open. "Gifts from my friends," I say.

"Pretty generous friends."

"The iPod is Joel's old one. He got a new one for Christmas." My brain finally wakes up. "Honey gave me the shirts."

"All of them?"

"What can I say?" I shrug, bury my face in my dinner plate.

"But you don't like this girl."

"I like her. Just not for a girlfriend." Dad's staring hard at me. I try not to squirm.

"You do like girls, don't you, son?"

My jaw drops and I look to see if he's ribbing me. He isn't. "Are you asking me if I'm gay?"

His expression is somber. "You're secretive. You don't seem to have your friends around much these days. I've spoken with Honey's mother and she said you never come over anymore. At Christmas, your aunt Debbie and I talked too."

"And for this you think I'm gay?" If he only knew how far from gay I am!

Dad's face gets red. "Look, I'm not condemning you. If you're gay—"

His broad-mindedness is laughable. I've heard him make jokes about gays. He wouldn't be so tolerant if I really were gay, no matter what he's saying now. And to think of him and Aunt Debbie sitting around her kitchen table discussing my sex life makes me crazy.

"How would you know what I do, where I go? You're always gone."

"I know what's going on in my own home, Ryan. Just because I'm not here a lot doesn't mean I don't keep tabs on you."

This causes my stomach to knot. What does he really know? "How? Reports from the housekeeper and cook? The lawn people?"

"Certainly Mrs. Gomez tells me that her workload is lighter than normal. And I can see that you hardly touch the food in the freezer. The neighbors talk to me too. You come and go a lot."

"You spy on me?" Now I'm shaking. Darn glad I've password-protected my computer.

"Don't make this about me," he says. "I'm your father and it's my responsibility to make sure you're safe, that you have a home, food—all the things you need."

"I need a car."

He waves me off. "You're not ready for a car. Not until I know what's going on with you."

"Nothing's going on with me. I'm just trying to get through high school. I have friends and I have a life."

He looks tired, and I see that he's trying to control his temper. "I care about you, son. I'm a single father who's doing the best I can. I don't want anything bad to happen to you. There's only one of me to parent you."

"So now it's my dead mother's fault?"

"Watch your mouth."

We never talk about Mom and I don't want to

now, but I was hoping to make him tell me what he knows and who the nosey neighbors are who are reporting to him. "I just don't like being spied on." My head hurts and my eyes burn. I push back from the table, scraping the chair across the floor, leaving a black mark on the tile. "I'm going to my room."

"We should talk this out."

"Why? I already know what you think of me." If I were reading a story in English class and my teacher asked me to give an example of irony, this would be the perfect one. I'm sleeping with one of my teachers and my father is asking if I'm gay. For a moment, I want to spew out the truth: *I'm banging a gorgeous woman who wants me all the time. Who can't get enough of me!*

"Come back here. I'm just trying to have a conversation with you. Make some connections and know you better."

I turn at the door. "Well, for the record, trust me when I tell you, I'm not gay."

I take the stairs to my room, two at a time.

Honey

I go up for a shot just as the halftime buzzer goes off, and the girl guarding me elbows me so hard in the side of the head, I see stars. The referee calls foul and while our opponents' coach argues the call, I try to shake off the pain. Mathers yells, "You all right, Fowler? Can you take the shots?"

I'm our best scorer from the foul line, so I tell him I can do it. We're down by two, so if I make the shots, we'll go into the locker room tied. I miss one, then get one, and we all head for the showers. On my way off the court, I look up at the half-filled bleachers to where my friends are sitting. Jess and Joel wave; so do Taylor and her new boyfriend, Wade. I stop short because Ryan is sitting up there too. And he's not with a girl.

I'm shocked because our season is half over and this is the first game he's made. He used to make all of them. He gives me a thumbs-up and I nod. All right! I have no idea why he's gracing us with his presence, but my heart beats faster because of it. Back on the court, I play my best. We win by five points, and I'm high scorer. Who says love can't inspire performance?

I rush through my shower and hurry out to where my friends are waiting. My pulse is racing, and I tell myself that Ryan won't be there. But he is.

"Great game!" Jess says. She and Taylor hug me. Joel and Wade add their praise too.

Ryan says, "Way to go."

"You noticed."

"Couldn't help noticing. You took it to them."

I give him a long look, wanting to forgive him for abandoning me, but not quite able to.

"We're heading out for food," Joel says. "Want to come, O Goddess of the Rim?"

Normally I'd say no, because who wants to hang around two happy face-sucking couples? Not me. But Ryan jumps in with "I'm in. Come on, Honey?"

"I'm in," I tell him.

"I have my dad's pimp-mobile. His old Caddy," Wade clarifies. "So there's plenty of room."

We head out the door of the gym and Ryan falls into step beside me. I ask, "Where have you been keeping yourself? I've missed seeing you at our games."

"Around. Busy with nothing in particular. No good excuse for missing your games. I'm sorry."

His apology sounds sincere, so I shrug. "Tonight

was our best game this season, so at least you saw a good one."

"You were hitting baskets. Pretty good for a freshman."

His grin infects me and I feel myself softening. "Coach doesn't have a choice. He has to use me. Lost too many seniors last June."

"Don't sell yourself short. You played good."

My heart swells because praise from Ryan counts ten times more to me than praise from any other person on Planet Earth.

He asks, "How's Cory doing?"

"Mom and Dad are sending him to a special school now. He's on campus five days a week and home on weekends."

"But he's just a kid. Only nine."

"He's ten, Ryan," I say softly. "Last November. You missed his party."

"I did?"

"I invited you. You didn't come."

Ryan goes quiet and when he finally speaks, he says, "Sorry. I'm saying that a lot tonight, aren't I? But I really am sorry."

"Cory asked for you. About a million times." A little fib, but I see that it hits home.

"What did you tell him?"

"I distracted him, same as I always do when his mind gets into a rut. Until he got over missing you."

Ryan says, "Maybe I can come over on a weekend. When he's home."

"Maybe."

I think he's just saying that, and he won't really show up. I feel sad. The distance between us feels like an ocean. By now we're at Wade's car, so Jess, Joel, Ryan and I cram into the backseat. Wade turns on the radio and the others talk above the noise. But Ryan and I sit silent, our bodies shoved together, no warmth in the contact between us. No warmth at all.

Ryan

I'm still pissed when I tell Lori about my conversation with Dad. "Gay! He thinks I'm gay because I don't talk about girls or date anyone."

We're half dressed, wrapped in a blanket on her sofa. "Want me to write you a note telling him you aren't?" she asks.

I pull away, see that she's joking and settle back again. "He wouldn't believe it. He thinks I'm just a stupid kid."

"You're no kid," she says, kissing my neck and sending a shiver up my back. In some ways, I can't get enough of her. In other ways, I miss my old life, hanging with my friends, going to basketball games, nothing more on my mind than dating some hot chick like Patti Warner in my lit class.

"My friends are riding me too," I say.

"How so?"

"They keep wanting me to be more like the Ryan they used to know."

I want to tell her that I feel as if I've been cut in half and belong to two universes—half to the high school universe, half to hers. She and I used to talk more. I could pour out all my feelings to her and she'd soothe me, make me feel as if my thoughts and ideas mattered. Not so much these days.

She pats my bare leg. "Forget them. You don't need them. We have each other. Aren't I enough for you?"

I wish I had the guts to tell her I'm afraid of being totally cut off from all the other things that mattered in my life until she came along. I'm afraid to even mention going to the girls' basketball game on Friday night, then out for burgers and a movie. I do tell her, "You don't play basketball. I miss going to the games."

"We can go to the games."

"We can't sit together."

"Sure we can. We just can't hold hands." She playfully tugs my ear and blows into it.

I pull aside. "I'm serious. People are starting to wonder about me and why I never show up for school events. They keep riding me about keeping secrets from them."

"They're self-centered, Ryan. They want you to be at their beck and call. Don't give in to them."

I could remind her that the two of us sure keep

secrets from each other. She hates her family, can hardly speak about her dad without going into a blue funk. Makes me realize that mine might not be so bad. I don't know what her dad did to her—she won't say—but somehow her mother is involved and Lori hates her, too.

Lori can be warm and sexy. She can also be cold and possessive. I don't get her, and when she goes in that dark direction, I want to go back to my other world, where things aren't as confusing and complicated.

"I'm just saying that I could spend a little more time with my friends. Make them back off with all their questions. 'Why don't you hang with us? Why aren't you around more? Why don't you come to games, or over to my house, or have us over for movies and video games?'" I repeat the list of questions I hear most often.

"And what do you want?"

Her eyes have turned all wary and I know I'm on thin ice, but I suck it up and say, "Maybe we should back off a little. Just until I can get back into my groove with my friends so they'll stop hounding me."

She straightens and stares hard at me. "Why are they so important to you? Can they give you what I can?"

"No, of course not." This isn't going as well as I'd

hoped. "My dad's got neighbors spying on me, and what if someone sees us together?" I know one of her worst fears is that we'll get caught.

"We're careful."

"Sure, but it only takes slipping up one time."

"But we're not going to slip up. We have each other. Damn your friends." She stands abruptly, taking the blanket, leaving me naked.

"Hey!" I grab at the blanket. "I'm cold."

"Me too, Ryan," she says. "You make my insides cold when you talk about dumping me."

"I never said that."

"It's what you mean. You think I can't read between the lines? You want to prove to your dad you're not gay. You want to prove to your friends that you're the same guy you used to be. And how do you do that? Why, by bringing home pretty little girls for them to inspect and then declare you 'normal.' You'd rather be with those empty-headed little teen twits than with me."

"I never—"

"We belong together. You and me—together. Lori and Ryan. Forever. I've given you everything, every inch of my body. All of my heart. And now you want to throw me away?" She starts to cry and I sit stupefied, my brain spinning, unable to follow her logic.

"I love you," she says. "I thought you loved me."

It makes me feel squirmy whenever she uses the "l" word, and she's been saying it more and more lately.

"You do love me, don't you, Ryan? Tell me you love me."

Her face looks blotchy and I don't want her to freak out. I leap up and grab her and hold her against me so she's locked in my arms and can't move. Just the way I've seen Honey do to Cory when he gets out of control. "Hey, calm down. You're always my number one. Of course I love you. How can you think I don't?"

The blanket feels warm and soft on my skin, but I'm still cold. I feel her body relax and soon she stops crying.

"I don't know what I'd do without you," she says. Her voice is husky and raw-sounding. "I just love you so much."

"Me too," I say, staring over her head and out the window at the tops of trees and open blue sky.

"Come to bed with me," she says.

And because I don't know what else to do, I go.

Lori

I'm awake again at three in the morning. I reach across the bed for Ryan, but he's not there. He hasn't spent a night with me for a couple of weeks, and I miss him. His father isn't traveling as much, so he's been pinned in place at his house. No more sneaking out after midnight, then back in before five the way he used to. I miss parking and waiting at the end of his street, my heart pounding with anticipation until I'd see him coming down the sidewalk, dressed all in black. He'd get into my car and after a quick hug we'd hurry back to my place for a few hours together.

Now I'm alone.

I know that a night is only several hours long, but it always seems longer when I'm alone in the dark. I send Ryan an e-mail telling him how much I miss him and what I'd be doing to him if he were here. Cyberspace is a poor substitute for flesh and blood.

Only a few more hours before I see him in class. This comforts me. Be patient.

He's restless. I see that. He's chafing against the rules we must obey. I can't change it. Not yet, anyhow, but someday . . .

I don't want us to get caught. It will ruin everything and take him away from me. The powers that be will throw me to the wolves. They'll come after me as if I were raw meat. And they'll surround Ryan like a pack of animals protecting their own from a bird of prey. I know what they'll think of me, what they'll call me, do to me. I don't care. Ryan's worth it. He still intrigues me, makes me want him even after all these months. I can't lose him. I can't.

Ryan

I've been lying to Lori. I've been telling her that Dad's traveling less. It's not true, but lately I've gotten a wake-up call about my grades. Failed two tests and am pulling Cs and Ds in every class except Lori's. She's giving me an A, but not because we're lovers—I'm actually working in her class. That idea is still hard for me to get my head around sometimes. Me and Ms. Settles, doing each other every chance we get.

Lori helps me with papers and assignments, but with tests I'm on my own. Dad will put me under house arrest if my grades don't come up. If I tell Lori I need to buckle down, she'll find a way to talk me out of it. She has in the past.

And then there's the problem of my friends. Lori just doesn't get it. I need to hang with them more. First because I want to, and second because I need to. They don't analyze every word I say. Or have a breakdown if I want to do something they don't want to do. Only thing is, when we go out and do stuff together, I feel as if I'm cheating on Lori. Not that I'm doing the horizontal boogie with anyone except her, but she can make me feel pretty guilty when she turns on the tears.

The guys tell me it's great to have me in the mix again. Honey acts as if I'm some long-lost traveler home from a faraway galaxy. One afternoon when I'm at her house, she tells me, "It's like you were lobotomized and now you're back. I've missed you."

"Sure," I say. "I was taken over by aliens, grown in a pod and tossed back into McAllister armed with only my wits. Bet you can hardly see the place where I was attached to my pea pod." I lift my shirt and show my belly button. Her face turns red, and I realize she's not like Lori, always wanting me naked. I pull down my shirt. "Sorry."

"What? You think I don't know you have a navel? We've been to the pool together, mister."

"Hey, chill. I was making a joke."

"I'm not mad. And I'm not a prude." She's all huffy-sounding.

I laugh. "Could have fooled me." I duck down, stare up at her face. "Whoa. Is that a flicker of a smile?"

She tries hard to hide it.

"Maybe this will help loosen it up." I spring on her, toss her onto the rec-room sofa and start tickling her.

In seconds, she's shrieking. "Stop it!" She's laughing and hiccupping, twisting and turning, but I keep up my tickle attack.

I shout, "My pod masters have given me the strength of ten bags of spinach. Resistance is futile!"

When she goes limp, I'm straddling her body and I've pinned her arms above her head. Her hair's a mess and she's breathing hard. Her face is as pink as if she's just played a game on the courts.

"You will pay!" she threatens, catching her breath and still laughing. "I will hurt you."

Watching her struggle, I feel a surge of power, and something comes over me I can't explain. Without thinking, I dip my head and kiss her on the mouth. I pull back and her eyes are wide and she's staring up at me like a startled bird. I roll off her as fast as I can and stand up. "Sorry."

"No. No, don't be sorry," she says.

But I hardly hear her because I'm already halfway up the stairs and heading for her front door.

Honey

Ryan kissed me. Me, Honey Fowler. On my mouth. Without any begging or pleading on my part, Ryan kissed me. I may never come down from the high I'm on. I won't tell anyone, not even Jess, because I want to hold on to the kiss and the feelings in my heart forever. If I share the story, my friends will dissect it, pick it apart and make it into something else.

"He likes you," Jess will insist.

"Finally he's come around," Taylor will say. "About time, too. How long have you crushed on him? A hundred years?"

I'll keep the magic to myself. Right here inside my heart, where no one can go except me. The kiss was spontaneous. He might not have planned it, but I have longed for it and now it's mine. He can't take it back.

I wonder if he really meant it. If he did, why did he apologize for doing it? A guy doesn't tell a girl he's sorry for stealing a kiss. Not if he really means it. I don't want him to be sorry. I want him to like me— love me—as much as I love him.

"What are you so happy about?" Jess stops me in the hall. She's tacking up posters for the upcoming freshman-sophomore spring dance.

"Do I look happy?"

"Air-walking happy."

"I'll try to look more serious."

She eyes me skeptically. "Something's different."

"I aced an algebra test."

"You do that all the time. No, this is something else."

"You're so nosey. Can't a girl just be happy without the third degree?"

"No."

I burst out laughing.

"What's so funny?" Joel has come up, slipped his arm around Jess.

"You're way too young to understand," I tell him, and turn and walk away.

When I see Ryan alone in the library later in the week, I freeze. What should I say? He looks up, beckons me over. I slide into the chair across from him at the table. "Are you a role model for Homeworkers Anonymous? You're always in the library."

He shrugs. "Got to keep up the grades. Better to do it here. Fewer distractions."

He's never had trouble before with his grades, but my mind isn't on schoolwork. "I haven't heard much from you lately." I choose my words. I want to ask, "Why haven't you called, or e-mailed, since you kissed me?"

"Full slate."

I stare at him, my heart pounding. "Too full to even shoot off an e-mail?"

"I haven't done a lot of things I used to do lately. Nothing personal."

I feel as if he's blowing me off. "I miss talking to you."

He lays down his pen, leans back in the chair. "Why are my friends giving me heat? You, Joel— I have a list. You all act like I don't care anymore just because I have to keep on the books. I'm working hard. I don't have time to explain every time I can't get together."

I feel stung, as if I'm messing where I'm not wanted. The kiss was a fluke. "I'll leave you to your books." I go to stand, but Ryan takes my wrist.

"Wait."

I sit.

"I'm not avoiding you. You're my best friend." His voice is softer.

I want to be more than your friend. "Okay. So now what?"

He tips his head and grins. "So why don't we go to the spring dance together?"

Ryan

What was I thinking? Why did I kiss Honey? Why did I ask her to the dance? To keep from having to talk about the kiss. I answer my own question. The kiss was an impulse. It just happened. I did it just because I could. Because Lori makes me crazy and I wanted to be in contact with my other world again. Stupid! But now I'm committed to going—Joel's already said we'll double—so backing out isn't an option.

I tell my dad, "I need some funds for the school dance at the end of the month."

"You're going?"

"Thought I would."

"That's great, son. Who are you taking?"

"Honey. We're doubling with Joel and Jess."

"Has something changed between you two?"

"Still just friends."

"And she's all right with that?"

"Seems to be."

He clears his throat. "Then have a good time."

"We will."

Before I can escape he says, "Ryan, I'm not prying, but I'm honestly interested in what's going on in your life. Because I'm gone so much, I feel more like a shadow around here than your father. We never talk about much when I am home, so I ask questions to get a dialogue going, not to pry."

"Okay." I shove my hands into the pockets of my jeans. I'm not in the mood for this. What does he expect me to say?

"Girls, grades and sports—guy stuff, right, son?"

He's trying too hard. I'm not into sports, my grades suck, and how can I ever tell him about my "girl"? "Dad, I'm doing fine. Don't worry about me."

"I'm not worried. It's just that we seem out of touch with each other. I chalk it up to you being sixteen and me being forty-seven, eh?"

"Dad, we haven't got any problems. My life's just not that interesting."

He waves me off. "Frankly, I'm glad you're taking the dating scene nice and slow. You're smart. It hasn't been easy for you growing up without a mother."

He surprises me, because we never talk about her. Or about what she did. "It doesn't bother me anymore," I say. "I got over not having her around a long time ago."

His mouth forms a hard line. "She shouldn't have left us," he says.

"But she did."

He reaches for his wallet, pulls out a few bills and hands them to me. "Enjoy the dance."

I slip out of the house at midnight and Lori meets me at the end of the block. She's talkative during the drive. I'm glad because it means she's in a good mood, and she won't be once I drop my bomb. As soon as we're inside her apartment, she wraps her arms around me. We kiss, then I step back from her embrace. "Listen, I have to tell you something."

"What is it?"

I tell her about the dance and taking Honey, adding, "I got backed into going, so don't get all frantic about it. It just happened and I have to do it."

"Why would I get frantic?"

"I don't know. . . . I just thought—"

"You're a high school freshman, Ryan. You made your case to me that sometimes you have to pick up your old life. I understand."

Lori doesn't go off on a crying jag. This is easier than I'd expected.

"Go to the dance with that big horsey girl and have a golly-gosh good time." She pats my cheek.

I should defend Honey. I don't.

"But you have to do something for me."

"Like what?"

"Next Friday is a teachers' work day. You're out of classes. I don't intend to show up for work. I want us to spend the day in Savannah. It's only a few hours from Atlanta and we can actually walk around in the open where no one knows us."

I'd planned to spend the day at Atlanta Underground, a cool hangout not far from home, with my friends. But I get that it's a trade-off—I get to go to the dance without a Lori scene, and she gets to go to Savannah with me in tow. It's worth it.

"All right," I tell her. "It's a deal."

Honey

"This is cool," Jess says, holding up a dress that glitters with gold sequins.

"It shouts 'hooker!'" Taylor says, pulling a simple green high-neck dress from the rack. "This is better."

I look at my friends, hardly believing that this time I'm the one we're shopping for. That I'm the one Ryan has asked to the McAllister freshman-sophomore dance.

"Fine," Jess snaps. "Send her out looking like her grandmother."

"A movie star would wear this in a heartbeat," Taylor says. "This is a happening dress."

"Boring," Jess says with a fake yawn. "An instant catnap. She needs to wow him, not put him to sleep."

"Hey, hey." I step between my two friends. "No fighting. This is supposed to be fun."

"I'm having fun," Taylor says. "Are you having fun?"

"I'm hysterical," Jess says.

We burst out laughing. It's a teachers' workday and we're at the mall searching for the perfect dress. My friends are happy for me, and I'm happy too. But I know this date with Ryan isn't like a regular boyfriend-girlfriend thing. It's not as if he calls me for no reason, or cozies up to me at school, or comes by my house just to be with me. Ryan doesn't treat me the way Joel treats Jess, or Wade treats Taylor. I'm not complaining. I'll take what I can get.

"Here it is!" Taylor says, triumphantly pulling a long bright-blue dress off a rack. She holds it up and we all stare in awe. The dress is beautiful, perfect for me—simple, and more elegant than sexy.

The color matches Ryan's eyes, I think. "You've got something there," I say. "Now let's hope it fits."

I clutch the dress and the three of us rush into a fitting room.

Ryan

Lori and I have a blast in Savannah. She's happy all day and we laugh a lot and spend a ton of her money. She takes me shopping and buys me the newest and best gaming console on the market, plus a stack of games and CDs. She picks out really cool clothes for me at some men's store where the salesguy is wearing a pink dress shirt and a red silk tie. The suits are Italian linen and silk and the casual shirts and pants cost in the triple digits. Way out of my league!

We stick the bags in the trunk of the car and I tell her, "I can't take all this stuff home. Too many questions."

"I'll keep the game box and most of the games at my place and you can use them when you come over. Problem solved."

I figure I can hide the clothes in the back of my closet and pull out a shirt once in a while. I do my own laundry, so Dad won't notice the new stuff. I won't make the same mistake I made at Christmas. "That'll work."

She's rented a convertible for the day, and driving with the top down makes talking difficult. Not a problem for me—I don't really want to talk, just blast down the open highway chasing the wind. On the trip home, Lori lets me drive. "You sure?" I ask, hopping into the driver's seat.

"Just don't get stopped by a cop." She ties a scarf around her hair.

"Oh, baby!" I say, and zip onto the interstate, feeling the power of the engine through my hands on the steering wheel.

By the time we hit Atlanta, afternoon has faded into evening and traffic is thinner. We're at her place in no time. Upstairs, she kisses me. I drop the packages and kiss her back, really kiss her, because the day has rocked.

"Can you stay?" she asks.

"Dad made me promise to be home by nine."

"But tomorrow's Saturday."

"Can't help it. I said I'd be there. He's putting pressure on me lately. Wants to be my buddy."

She rolls her eyes, and for a minute I think she's going to pitch a fit. I'm relieved when she finally says, "All right. I'll run you home."

I gather up a couple of the new games to take with me. The clothes are still in the trunk. "Let's go."

"You ready for the dance next Friday?" she asks while driving.

I've come to be suspicious about her casual questions. "I'm ready. Why?"

"I just want to tell you that I've volunteered to chaperone."

We've been together all day and she's just now telling me this? "Okay."

"I'm not checking up on you, Ryan, if that's what you're thinking. Dexter asked for faculty volunteers and I never do anything to help out, so this seemed like a good way to stay in her good graces."

"You're in her good graces now?"

"Ever since I've been dressing like a frump. I'm not even on her radar."

The longer skirts and flats haven't fooled anyone. Every guy in school knows the kind of body her clothes are covering. Me most of all. "Whatever it takes to keep our principal happy," I say.

Two blocks from my house, she rolls to the curb. I make for the door, but she stops me.

"You had a good time today, didn't you?"

"I had a great time."

"Good." Her smile is cheerful. "I want you to always have a good time with me."

I watch her drive off. Then I jog home, where Dad's waiting to grill me about my day at the Underground.

. . .

The problem with a high school dance in the gym is that it's so . . . well, so high school. The pep club has decorated the place with murals, glitter and balloons, but it's still a gym. A disc jockey, a senior who has a part-time job at a local radio station, is spinning tunes onstage, and whirling rainbow-colored lights are spraying the room and the mob of kids who've shown up with bright colors.

I'm glad I came. For the first time in a long time, I feel like my former self. Just Ryan. Honey looks good, too. I hadn't figured she'd be as pretty as she is tonight. When she first came down the stairs at her house, I took a step backward because she looked like a model or something.

Truth is, all the girls look pretty, even the ones who seem ordinary in classrooms and halls.

"Whoa!" Joel says. "Look thataway."

We all turn and my heart lurches. Lori's standing there and Coach Mathers is practically slobbering on her. She's wearing a short, low-cut black dress and superhigh heels that sparkle in the lights.

Taylor grabs Jess and Honey. "Come on. Let's get a close-up. I'll bet ten bucks that dress is designer. I swear I saw it in *Vogue*."

"I'd rather not," Honey says, holding back, but Taylor won't be put off.

The three of us guys trail after our dates, me last

because I don't know how to act around Lori. Not in front of everybody.

"Hello, Ms. Settles," Taylor gushes. "You look fab!"

"Thank you, Taylor. All you girls are lovely." She's using her soft teacher voice, her eyes warm and friendly. She doesn't even look my way.

"Hey, Coach," Honey says.

"My star player," he says to Lori.

"So I've heard," Lori says. "You're one heck of a basketball player, according to the newspaper. Good for you. Girl power."

Honey smiles, but I know she doesn't like being singled out. And I know she doesn't like Ms. Settles. She squints and I notice that she's looking hard at Lori's throat. "That's a pretty necklace," she says.

Lori touches the silver knot on the hammered silver chain resting against her skin. "Thank you. It was a gift from a friend. For Christmas."

Taylor and Jess agree that the necklace I gave Lori is "really pretty." It surprises me that she's wearing it, but so what? No one knows who gave it to her.

"You all have fun," Lori says, and she and Coach walk toward the food tables.

A slow song begins to play and Taylor and Wade peel off to the dance floor. Honey turns to me and she's white as a ghost. "You okay?" I ask.

"Just a little sick to my stomach," she says. "I didn't eat dinner."

Sure came on sudden, I think.

Jess grabs her arm. "To the girls' room. We'll see you guys in a few minutes."

I watch them weave through the dancers, the lights reflecting bright spots of color off the backs of their dresses and hair until they disappear into the shadows on the far side of the gym.

Honey

The bathroom is foggy with hair spray. Girls are preening at the mirrors, smearing on lip gloss and gobs of mascara. The mix of so many different perfumes makes me more nauseated, and I rush into an empty stall, lock the door and lean against the cool metal wall, fighting for control.

Jess bangs on the door. "You okay?"

"I will be," I lie. My stomach is churning, my heart beating hard. When I close my eyes, all I see is Lori Settles' necklace—the Celtic love knot on its silver chain nestled at her throat. A Christmas gift from a friend.

"Want me to go get you something to eat?" Jess asks.

"No. I—I don't want to throw up."

"Bad news. How about some cola?"

"Not now."

I take deep breaths, force myself to calm down.

I've seen that style of necklace twice, once here in Atlanta. Whoever gave it to Settles could have bought it right here in the city. And once in a velvet box in Ryan's room.

"Do you need to go home?" Jess again.

"I don't know yet."

I hear the voices of other girls saying, "What's up with Honey?" and "Is she all right?"

"Stomach bug," Jess says.

No germs, I think—fear. My legs feel wobbly. "How about a wet paper towel," I say to keep Jess busy. I need time to think. Why would Ryan give Lori Settles a necklace? A bribe for grades? Stupid. I discard that notion quickly. Why? I can't face the ugly thought that keeps banging against the inside of my head.

"Incoming," Jess says, passing a soggy wad of paper towels under the door of the stall.

I take them, wring them out into the toilet and press them to the back of my neck. The cold feels good and revives me. I do more deep breathing. You're being stupid, I tell myself. I'm letting it ruin my night. There are plenty of people who could have given Settles her necklace. Maybe even Coach. Or a friend from her past. Or one of those firemen from that time we worked the carnival. I remember how a few of them were falling over themselves to talk to her. I'm betting the necklace Ryan bought is still in his room.

"Status report," Jess says.

"Better," I say, getting a handle on my emotions. "I'm coming out." I unlock the door and step out into a circle of curious girls.

"Show's over," Jess tells them. "Scram."

They scatter and I walk to the mirror. At least I didn't cry, so my mascara's in place. I fumble for lip gloss, smear it on.

"Whatever it was, I'm over it," I say.

"Probably your period," Jess says. "Sometimes just before I start, it knocks me out."

"You're probably right," I tell her. "Mother Nature can be a royal pain."

Lori

They look so fresh-faced. The girls in their pretty party dresses. The boys in sports jackets or suits. I can tell none of the girls get dressed up much because their bodies aren't at ease with the swish of filmy fabrics, or the cut of strapless dresses over underwire bras, or the lift of high-heeled shoes. They walk stiff-legged, afraid of stumbling and making fools of themselves. But they are young, with smooth skin and girly laughs and all their hopes for love riding on goodnight kisses in the moonlight. So naive.

I watch the boys watching the girls. They can't keep their eyes off cleavage and soft shoulders and high, rounded butts. They push against their dance partners, pressing the shapes of the girls to accommodate their own, feeling bare skin and risking a quick kiss when they think we chaperones aren't watching. As if I'd step between them. Let them revel in their illusion of romance. It's over soon enough.

When Ryan arrives with the horsey girl in tow, my mouth goes dry. He looks delicious wearing a coat and tie, both bought by me. I want him to know the luxury of quality fabrics and well-cut clothes. He should know that the garment universe doesn't consist only of T-shirts and denim. The stretch of Italian linen across his shoulders, the slimness of his waist and narrow hips, excite me. He always makes me want him.

He's smiling at the girl and she's smiling back. Can he see how she feels about him? Does he know how much she wants him? If he's blind to her, I'm glad. I can't compete with her youth.

"Young love. Isn't it grand?" Coach Mathers interrupts my thoughts.

"Very grand," I say.

"I don't even remember being that young."

He's attempting to engage me in conversation, but I don't care to talk to him. He's a nonevent on my calendar. "I do."

After a few minutes of staring at the dancers, he asks, "So, are you finding your way around Atlanta well enough?"

"Yes."

"Took me a long time when I first moved here. Why do you suppose they named so many streets Peachtree?"

"Yes, that is peculiar."

He's annoying me. I want him to leave me alone. I turn and see Ryan and a group of his friends coming toward me. My nerve endings tingle. I was content to stay in the background tonight and out of his way because lately he's wanted to reconnect with these kids. I'm cool with that. Mostly because I think he'll tire of them quickly. Especially when he has me waiting for him.

I force myself not to look at Ryan. Two of the girls are in my classes, so it's easy to smile and talk to them. They admire my necklace. The girl Ryan's with, Honey, can't take her eyes off it. "A gift from a friend," I tell them, knowing they could never guess just how friendly Ryan and I are.

Once they walk away, I ask Mathers to get me a soda and he scurries off like a lovelorn puppy. The music is loud and the colored lights swirl across the dancers like smears of bright paint. I close my eyes and absorb the sound like a sponge. I was never this young. I should have been. But my father took it all away from me. And my mother did nothing to stop him. Not one damn thing.

Ryan

I'm awake in my room at two in the morning, restless, thinking that the dance was a big waste of time, when my computer signals that an urgent e-mail has hit my inbox. It's from Lori.

Did you like the dance? Was it all you wanted it to be? I thought you looked good enough to eat. . . .

The e-mail goes on to describe what she'd like us to be doing to each other right now, and all I want is to get into bed with her. My body aches. I need her. I feel ready to explode.

Want to come get me?

She replies:

Let me grab my keys and I'm on my way.

I dress in black, open a window and edge out onto the porch roof, then slide down a side column holding up the porch. I've made this escape many times to meet her, so I'm waiting at the end of my block when she drives up. I get into her car.

She reaches over, squeezes me, and I shiver. "I don't want to wait one more minute," she says. She drives to a nearby golf course and parks behind a clump of trees on the rough. I slide my seat as far back as it will go and she climbs on top of me. In minutes, our clothes are off and the insides of the windows are steamy. "I want you," she whispers. "I want you now."

When it's over, when we're both limp and gasping for breath, she buries her face in my chest. "For what it's worth, I hated seeing you with that girl."

"Neither of us had a good time," I say. "Honey got sick to her stomach and we just went through the motions the rest of the night."

"I'm sorry she got sick." Lori doesn't sound too convincing.

"Did you have a good time with Mathers?"

"He's not my type."

"Good. I didn't like seeing you with him, either."

She pulls back and the necklace I gave her catches a stray gleam of light. I touch it. "It looks good on you."

"Especially when it's all I'm wearing."

I grin. "Right."

Suddenly a beam of light hits our side window.

"What's going on in there?" a man's voice says. "You all right? Have an accident?"

I freeze. Lori rolls off me, scrambles into the driver's seat, cranks the engine.

"This is private property!" the voice shouts.

I make out the shape of a man in a uniform holding a flashlight. "Cops!" I tell Lori.

The man bangs on the window.

"A security guard," she says. "Hang on." She puts the car into reverse. The tires spin in the soft dirt and for a second I think we're stuck, but the tires grab on to hard clay and the car shoots backward.

The man yells, "Stop!"

The tires squeal as we hit pavement and the car fishtails, but Lori holds it and in seconds we're wheeling down a side street. My heart's racing, but I feel electrified, alive to the tenth power. Lori slows and we both let out a whoop. "Awesome!" I shout between fits of laughing.

"That was a close one." Lori pounds the steering wheel. "He ate our dust!"

We drive, and as the pumped feeling leaves me, I begin to sweat. "What if we'd been caught?"

"We weren't."

But my adrenaline is gone and all I want to do is get back to my room. "Better take me home."

"Better get dressed."

I've forgotten I don't have clothes on. I manage to

tug on my jeans, shirt and shoes while Lori drives slowly around for block after block. Once I'm dressed, she makes a turn onto my street and stops a few doors down from my house. I look over at her. "What about you? Want me to wait while you dress?"

She pulls an athletic jacket from the backseat and slips it on. "I'll finish when I hit my parking lot."

I grin. "Don't get pulled over by a cop."

She leans over and kisses me. "I love you, Ryan. You make me feel alive. I don't know what I'd do if I ever lost you."

I get out, jog through two yards to the barking of neighborhood dogs, shimmy up the porch column and scramble into the safety of my room. It's four in the morning when I collapse on my bed. I'm glad it's Saturday and I can sleep in.

Honey

Mom comes into my room around ten on Saturday and asks, "How was the dance?"

I've been awake for a long time but too depressed to get out of bed. I turn toward the wall. "Great time."

"I'm so glad. I heard you come in but thought I'd wait until this morning before getting a report."

"Later," I tell her, knowing there's only one thing to report and I'm still sorting it out.

Mom picks up my dress from the floor. "Honey, this dress cost a lot. Don't leave it wadded up this way."

"Sorry," I mumble.

She takes it to my closet and hangs it on the back of the door, fluffing and smoothing the shimmery fabric. "You and Ryan looked so good together last night. I've already downloaded the digital photos Dad took onto the computer. When you come down, take a look. You were glowing. Did Ryan have a good time?"

I can't tell Mom the truth—our date was a bust. That's what happens when you get your hopes up. A burst bubble. Ryan was bored. I was confused. All I could think about was Lori Settles and her necklace. Ugly thoughts. Hateful ideas. "You'll have to ask him," I say.

Mom stands beside my bed, and I feel her gaze on my back. "You feel all right?"

"I'm fine. Hungry." I toss back the covers. No use making Mom wonder what's going on with me. She has the instincts of a hawk, and wheedling power to boot.

"I saved you some pancake batter."

"I'll be right there," I say.

When she's gone, I crawl into sweatpants and a sweatshirt, find a scrunchie and pull my hair into a ponytail. I don't look in the mirror because I know what I look like—I'm big-boned and oversized and I have smudges of last night's mascara under my eyes. The real Honey Fowler. Across the room, the dress hangs on a padded hanger, sapphire blue and feminine, a curse from the night my dreams crashed and burned. I'll never wear it again.

I have to know the truth. It takes me a week to devise a plan. I wait for an afternoon when I know Ryan's not at home, when his dad's on the road, when their housekeeper is almost ready to finish her chores for the day. I ring Ryan's doorbell. When Mrs. Gomez opens the door, I say, "Hey there. Remember me—Honey Fowler?"

"Yes, Ryan's friend." She gives me a big smile. "Ryan's not here."

"Rats!" I act disappointed. "Listen, I really need a favor. He's got some material I need up in his room for a project I'm doing at school and it's due tomorrow. Can you please let me in so I can go up and find it? I promise I won't take long."

I see her hesitate.

"We can phone him on his cell," I say, hoping she won't call my bluff. "He's in the library, so he may not have it turned on."

She gives me a smile and steps aside. "I am sure this will be okay."

"Thanks!" I rush up the stairs and into his room, my palms sweating and my heart racing. Liar, liar! I hear my conscience shout.

His room is neat as a pin. A place for everything, and everything in its place. No velvet box in sight. He could have put it anywhere. I can't quite stoop to opening the dresser drawers and pawing through his things. Nothing on his desk, either. Just his computer. I go to his computer, remembering that it's password protected. I pray he hasn't changed the password since fifth grade, when we played computer games together.

He hasn't. I call up his e-mail program. I rummage through his inbox, outbox, deleted messages. Nothing. I hear Mrs. Gomez start the vacuum downstairs. Hurry, I tell myself.

Minutes later I find a subfolder inside a saved folder marked WORLD HISTORY with a list of e-mails from carnivaldaze. The folder is large and organized by date. Just like Ryan, I think. I choose one and read it, and almost go into shock. It's graphic, sexual and explicit. And Ryan's replies to this person's e-mails leave nothing to the imagination. I feel sick.

Below, the vacuum stops and Mrs. Gomez calls out, "Are you finished, Honey?"

"Almost!" I shout back. "Just five more minutes."

I find a stack of writable CDs on a shelf next to Ryan's computer. My fingers have lost all feeling and I almost drop the blank CD that I pick up. I slide it into the machine and copy the entire subfolder.

Back home, I run upstairs and lock my bedroom door, turn on my computer and with shaking hands insert the copied CD into the disk drive. When the list of files flashes onto the screen, I read them, starting from the earliest date to the one from as recent as the day before. I see the entire history of Ryan's relationship with carnivaldaze. He addresses her by name in several of the e-mails: *Lori*. No doubt remains in my mind that Lori Settles, *Ms. Settles,* is carnivaldaze and that she and Ryan are having an affair.

Bile rises into my mouth and I fight off the urge to vomit. Ryan and Lori. Student and teacher. Boy and woman. Friends with benefits. Lovers.

I exit the program, remove the CD and stash it between two books on a shelf. I wish I could wash out my brain and rid myself of the pictures the e-mails have imbedded in my mind. I wish I had never snooped. Too much information.

The pain is unbearable, the sense of betrayal stupefying. When I left Ryan's room an hour ago, I left my romantic notions behind, my idea of sex as something beautiful and meaningful between two people who love each other. I also left behind my hopes, my dreams, and my heart.

Honey

It feels as if worms are crawling around in my brain. I've read the e-mails about a hundred times over the past few days, and I'm convinced that Lori Settles is a monster and that Ryan is despicable. Worst of all, knowing what's going on between them has pulled my life out of shape and turned me into someone I don't like.

The secret I'm carrying around is eating me alive. I can't sleep. I've lost interest in school, and I blew our final game of the season so badly that Coach took me out at halftime and made me ride the bench. I don't care. I just want the pain inside me to stop.

"What's going on with you?" Jess asks after cornering me in the hall at my locker.

"Nothing. I've just had a lot on my mind."

"Everything all right at home? With your brother?"

"Cory's fine, and the parents are all right too."

"Then what? It's like you're off on a distant planet."

"Two huge papers due," I say.

Jess looks worried. I think about telling her what I know, but don't. I want to tell someone but don't know who to tell, or how.

"You just look so unhappy," Jess says. "I miss my friend."

Tears bubble up into my eyes. "I'll get on top of things," I tell her. "Back to normal soon." But it's not true. I don't even know what normal is anymore. My thoughts are torturing me. My feelings are over-whelming. I *want* to do something. I *have* to do something.

Cory comes home for Easter and I realize I've missed him. I envy him too, because the world he lives in isn't as complicated as mine, at least not when it comes to emotions. We're outside tossing a ball when Ryan and Joel drive by in Joel's car. They stop, come across the front lawn. Just seeing Ryan makes my stomach all queasy. I recall a time when it was jumpy every time I saw him—a time when every nerve in my body was lit up because he was near me. Knowing what I know now, I just feel sick.

Joel sits on the front step and gets on his cell. Ryan walks up to me and Cory.

"Hey, buddy," Ryan says to my brother.

Cory recognizes him, but he doesn't offer himself to be hugged. Autistic kids are that way—sometimes they want you, sometimes they don't. Sort of like Ryan, I think.

Cory walks away. "How's he doing?" Ryan asks me.

It's hard for me to speak to him, but since it's about Cory, I say, "He's doing good at that school. They think he can mainstream into third grade next year."

"That's great."

Cory wants me to toss him the ball. Ryan picks it up and rolls it to him. Cory lets it lie at his feet. "He wants me to do it," I say. I go, pick up the ball and hand it to Cory. He waits until I'm several feet away and rolls it to me.

"Guess I'm not his favorite pal anymore," Ryan says.

"Guess not," I say. Lurid pictures of Ryan and Lori run around in my head. My stomach roils.

"You mad at me?" Ryan asks. "Because you act mad."

"Did you catch up your grades?"

"Mostly. Still a little heat in math."

"But not in world history, I'll bet."

He gives me a funny look. "I do all right."

I'll bet you do, I think. I want to spew angry words at him. I want him to know that what he's doing is horrible. I want him to know how he's crushed me, how bad I'm hurting. I say nothing.

Joel comes off the porch. "Got to run, Ry."

Ryan hangs back. "I can walk home from here."

"No," I say. "Go on. I've got stuff to do."

He looks surprised. Probably never remembers a time I haven't begged him to stay. "Okay. I'll see you around."

I watch them drive away. I don't know how long I stand staring into space, but at some point I feel a tug on my sleeve. I look down at Cory. He reaches up and touches my cheek, pulls his hand away and stares at his finger. "Wet," he says.

I wipe my face. I've been crying without realizing it. I take the ball from his other hand and smash it hard into the ground.

Three days later I make up my mind. I know exactly what I'm going to do.

Ryan

We have a substitute teacher in world history today. I knew about her ahead of time because Lori called my cell last night and said she didn't feel good and was taking a sick day. I thought about cutting class, but I have a test next period, so what good will an hour of not being here get me? I sit and doodle on my notebook cover and wait for the bell to ring.

The door of the classroom opens and Mr. Sampson, our assistant principal, steps inside. Everyone looks up because it must be important if Sampson comes into a classroom. "May I help you?" the sub asks.

"Ryan Piccoli," Sampson says.

I bolt upright. Me? He wants me?

The guy in the seat behind me pokes me in the shoulder. "What did you do, man?"

"Ryan?" the sub asks, glancing around the room because she doesn't know who's who.

I stand. "Yes," I say.

"Come with me," Sampson says.

"What's up?" I ask the second we're in the hall.

"Mrs. Dexter's office" is all he tells me.

I'm racking my brain, trying to figure out what I did to get called to the office. A scary thought suddenly hits me. "Is it my dad? Did something happen—"

"Nothing like that," he says.

I feel momentary relief and then we're at the office and Sampson's taking me into Dexter's inner sanctum. She's there along with a man and a woman. I know in my gut that they're cops.

Dexter points to a chair. "Ryan, please sit down."

I ease into the chair and she introduces the two as Detectives Cole and Sanchez. Everyone's staring at me.

"Your father's out of town?" Dexter asks.

"Until tomorrow."

"Is there anyone you can stay with?"

"Why?"

"We want you in protective custody."

My brain's spinning. "Why?"

She opens a manila folder on her desk and hands me a single sheet of paper from a thick stack. I read the first few words and right away I know what's going on. They've found out about me and Lori. My stomach heaves and I start to sweat. I'm scared.

"These detectives are going to arrest her, Ryan. She's going to jail."

"But—"

I struggle to stand, but one cop, Sanchez, I think, puts his hand on my shoulder. "Stay put, son."

"Is she in trouble?"

"You're not in trouble, but she's perpetrated a crime," Sanchez says.

My head's spinning and all I want to do is run. "No crime. I—I wanted to be with her."

"She's a predator, Ryan. A sexual predator." Dexter's face looks pale. "She's taken terrible advantage of you. And you're not the first young man she has a sexual history with, either. Not the first, but if I can help it, you'll be the last."

PART
3

Ryan

The people in Dexter's office keep talking to me. I see their lips moving, but I'm not listening. All I hear over and over is Dexter's voice: ". . . And you're not the first young man she has a sexual history with, either." I think about all the times Lori's said she loves me. I thought I was special, the first.

At some point I ask, "Can I go get my stuff from my class?"

"I'll go with you," Sampson says.

I don't argue, just try to figure a way to lose him. We head down the hall and I catch a break when the bell rings and the hall fills up. Since he isn't holding on to me, I duck and slither between groups of jabbering girls.

"Hey!" he yells.

Startled, the girls look at Sampson and stop walking. Without meaning to, they block him and I break away. I dash down a hallway to where Joel's next class is meeting and catch him at the door. "Keys," I say.

"What's the matter?"

"Now!"

He hands over his car keys. "What's—"

I hear nothing more because I'm hitting an exit door and running to the parking lot.

I pound on Lori's door and when she opens it, I shove my way inside.

"Ryan! What's wrong?"

"They know about us."

"What?" All the color leaves her face.

"Dexter dragged me into her office and there were cops, too."

"But how—"

"She had a whole stack of e-mails. The ones we sent each other."

"You didn't erase them?"

"I filed them," I say. "Password-protected everything. I don't know how this happened." I go into her kitchen. There are a big pot boiling on the stove and chopped vegetables lying on a cutting board.

"Oh my God." She sags against the counter. "You should have erased them. Why did you save them?"

The tone of her voice is like a hard slap—a teacher's voice scolding me. "Don't put this on me. I liked to read them to be nearer to you."

"I'm sorry, baby. I—I didn't mean to yell at you. This is terrible. Really bad."

I cut her off. "Dexter said there were others. Like me. Other guys."

It takes her seconds to speak and in that stretch, I know it's true. "That's not the way it was, Ryan. It's just the spin she wants to put on it." Lori reaches for me, but I jerk away.

"Was I your first?" I'm shouting. "I assumed I was your first!"

She goes quiet and the look on her face tells me everything. "But you're the one I love."

"I was just a lay, wasn't I? Just a f—"

She puts her hand over my mouth. "Don't say it. Don't make it dirty. I love you."

I break away. "I've been stupid. Why did I believe you?"

I turn, but she grabs me. "Don't leave. I need you."

"Tell me about the others. I want to know about all the others."

She's crying and she picks up the big chopping knife and begins to chop carrots furiously, attacking them as if they're an enemy. "No others. Just one. A boy who needed me. His parents were destroying him, pressuring him to be someone they wanted him to be and not who he was. He was so needy."

I can't believe what I'm hearing. "So you were helping him?"

"Don't you get the difference? He needed me, but I need you!"

My head's spinning, and the walls seem to be closing in on me. Women in my life have been my friends' mothers, or teachers, or Dad's girlfriends, or neighbors. I don't know how they behave or think. Lori's the only woman who's shown an interest in me. I feel trapped and confused. "I've got to get out of here," I say.

"You can't go. Don't leave me."

A pounding on the front door makes us both jump. "Lori Settles, please open the door. This is the police."

Lori clutches my arm. She looks like a cornered animal. My heart's pounding like a jackhammer. On the stove the boiling pot throws moisture onto the burner and it sizzles. Hot steam hits the cool air.

"Open up." The command comes again through the door.

I unlatch Lori's fingers from my arm and back away. There's only one way out and that's through the door. I head for it, hear a cry and then the clatter of something hitting the floor behind me. I spin and see Lori bent over, the big chopping knife on the tile, and blood gushing down her wrist and hand. I shout, "No!" and grab her before she drops to the floor. "What are you doing?"

She folds over like a broken doll while I'm holding

her. We slide down together and I hug her against my body while her blood gushes and the pounding on the door grows frantic. I lift her arm upward, watch her blood pour in a steady stream of red.

I'm crying, "Stop! Stop!" as if I can stem the flow by words alone. My back is braced against the refrigerator, and I feel a dishtowel hanging from the handle. I snatch the cloth and wrap it tight around her wrist, too tight, because she cries in pain and keeps begging over and over, "Let me die, Ryan! Please let me die!" and then the front door splinters open and people come through the kitchen doorway like roaches and I say to Lori, "You can't die! Not like this. Not the way my mother did it."

Ryan

' 'Fallout." It's a word used to describe the after-effects of a nuclear event. The perfect word to describe the aftermath of me and Lori. Most of that afternoon is a blur—a fast-forwarded DVD where people move like speeded-up robots. I recall cops, paramedics, nosey neighbors, an ambulance at Lori's complex. I remember someone peeling me off her, putting her on a stretcher and rolling her away. I remember her blood soaked into my jeans and shirt. I remember some social-service woman taking me into custody and waiting for my father, and him catching the first available plane and showing up at the police station and taking me home, and having to see the events revisited on the evening news and only then learning that Lori had been treated for her injury in the ER, released and taken to jail.

Some of the fallout was explosive, like my dad getting in my face once he knew I was safe, shouting questions and accusations at me. "An affair with your teacher? My God, Ryan, what were you thinking?"

"It wasn't like that. We loved each other."

"Love! You're a kid! What could she see in you? You're just a kid!"

That went all over me. "She didn't think so."

"Are you that deluded? Where is your brain? Don't answer!" he roared. "At sixteen, your brain's in your pants. That's what she liked about you. She's sick. She's perverted. A child molester. I'll see to it that she goes to jail for the rest of her life."

I go berserk when he says that. I call him names and he yanks me off the sofa and shoves me toward my room, where I sit, cut off from everybody and every form of communication—no cell phone, no computer, no friends, even no school for a week. My father says I need help. What does he know? I can't go out of the house because reporters are hanging around. I can't watch TV without seeing and hearing talking heads commenting on Lori and her "boy lover." I almost go stir-crazy. But it gives me time to think.

I think about Lori, about her all alone in jail and being vilified by the news media and hated by everyone. I miss her body. I wanted her from the start. What a difference she made in my life, and I am not sorry I was with her. I think how much I want things back the way they used to be. I think about the other guy, too. Who was he? And did she really not love him the way she said she loves me?

I think about my mother. I go through old photos, wondering why she did what she did. When I was twelve, Aunt Debbie came for a short visit and I begged her to tell me how my mother "did it." I'd been curious about her suicide for years, and Dad would only say, "You were just a little guy. No need to hear the details."

Aunt Debbie said, "You should ask your father."

"He won't talk about it. He tells me nothing."

"I told Bill years ago that he should tell you everything."

"But he hasn't. Aunt Debbie, please. I have to know."

"Jane was troubled and unhappy. I could never figure why. She had people who loved her, a nice home, a good husband, a lovely son. In the end it wasn't enough. She left you with a good neighbor one afternoon, went home, locked the bathroom door, drew a bath and got into the tub. She slit her wrists and bled out into the water. Your father found her dead when he got home that afternoon, and she left no note. We'll never know why she did it."

I flip through the old pictures. My mother was pretty, but her eyes look sad in every photo. How unhappy does a person have to be to kill herself? She didn't love me enough to stick around. What kind of mother leaves her two-year-old to grow up without her?

When, in another fight with Dad, I compare what Lori and Mom did, he loses it. He insists that Lori cut herself for dramatic effect and to get sympathy, but when I ask how that's different from what Mom did, he says, "Don't ever compare your mother with that slut," and balls up his fists. For a second I think he's going to slug me, but he leaves the room and slams the door.

The other thing I think about is how Dexter got hold of my private e-mails. Someone gave them to her, but who? Lori and I were careful. I kept my mouth shut to everybody, even Joel, who's so wrapped up with Jess that he hardly knows right from left, proving to me that he's not getting any sex. When a guy's not into full-time thinking about getting his rocks off, he concentrates on other things. I did. Pulled up my low grades in six weeks because Lori quenched the fire inside me that never goes away. When we were climbing into the sack regularly, it became a controlled blaze. I wish we could do it again right now.

Maybe Coach Mathers found out. No secret that he wanted Lori all to himself, so maybe he outed us. But I discard that idea because he has no access to my computer.

So I spend long stretches of time alone, turning the

question over in my mind, looking at it from every angle. In the end, I come down to one conclusion. There's only one person who could have discovered the truth about me and Lori. Only one. Honey Fowler. Something was different about her after the dance. She wasn't the same. I can't figure out why she did it, though. That's the mystery that's driving me nuts.

Honey

What have I done? The world has exploded and it's my fault. Lori Settles is in jail. Ryan's under house arrest and then who knows what will happen to him? Reporters are crawling all over the place, and no one at school can talk about anything except Ryan and Settles and their affair. My parents won't allow me to talk to anyone except Jess and Taylor, and I don't want to talk to them because they'd ask too many questions—"Did you know? Who blew their cover? How long do you think Ryan's been doing Lori? Are you sure you're clueless about this?" With the push of a computer key, I created this tornado of badness. I sent the e-mail folder I copied from Ryan's computer to Mrs. Dexter and now life as I once knew it is over.

I insist I don't know anything, but inside I'm dying. Joel swears he didn't know about it either, and I'm sure that's true. Ryan was the perfect liar. He hid everything from us in plain sight. While we went to school games and pep rallies and giggled in the halls, Ryan went to bed with Lori, a woman seventeen years older than him. While I sat on the sidelines of his life—wishing, longing, praying for him to be with me—he was meeting Lori secretly. I wanted him so much—me, Honey, the unlovely one, the gal-pal from elementary school, the girl down the street, the one who loved him from afar but could never have him.

I hate him now. As much as I once loved him, I now hate him. Swear to God.

Mom's been grilling me. "Did Ryan ever try anything with you?"

"Never," I say. Imagine if she knew that I'd raided his room and turned him in. "Never," I repeat.

"Because if he did, I want to know, Honey. You don't have to protect him."

"I'm not protecting him. We've only been friends."

"Some friend. Actually, your father and I don't truly blame him. He's a horny teenage boy, and boys will take whatever they can get. That vile Lori woman was willing to take his innocence. That's who we blame. I get the shivers just thinking about how she took advantage of Ryan."

"I think he liked it, Mom."

She makes a face. "Disgusting. Of course he liked it. But the newspeople say that Ryan wasn't her first victim. There was another boy, back in Chicago where she taught before coming to McAllister. He was only fourteen and his parents didn't want it dragged through the media."

I've seen all the newscasts, read every newspaper story, and there was no hard evidence against Lori and the other boy, just rumors. The boy denied it and so did she. "No proof, Mom," I say. "Just hearsay." Not like the proof the authorities have on her and Ryan, I remind myself.

"More of a shame. The files were closed and poor Mrs. Dexter had no clue she was hiring a predator." I hide behind a magazine when she adds, "I wonder who blew the whistle this time? Whoever it was deserves a medal." Mom shakes her head with a dramatic sigh. "The pity is that this Lori creature will get a fancy lawyer and be out in no time. That's my prediction."

I wake up from a deep sleep to the sound of someone calling my name from outside our walk-in basement's patio doors. It's very late on a Saturday night and I've fallen asleep on the sofa watching a movie. I sit up and turn toward the sound and see Ryan through the glass. My heart jumps into my throat.

Ryan says, "Let me in."

"Go away."

"I'm not leaving until we talk."

"I'm getting my father." I make a move toward the stairs.

"No. You're going to talk to me because I know what you did."

I freeze.

"Please," he says.

I loathe myself, but I go to the sliding doors and open one and he steps into the room. I close the door after him. Even now, my heart is pounding and a part of me is so glad to see him. Then all the memories, all his dirty e-mails and my lewd imaginary pictures of him with Lori doing the nasty, slam into my brain. "What do you want?"

"I want to know why you went to Dexter."

I immediately search for a way to deny I was the one, but I know he won't believe me. I want to hurt him the way he's hurt me. "Because what the two of you were doing was wrong! Because you're a dirty liar and you let her use you!"

"We weren't hurting anybody. It was private, just between me and Lori."

"You're sixteen, Ryan."

"And we don't know any sixteen-year-olds doing the deed, hooking up and humping in parked cars? Come on!"

"But they're doing it with kids their age."

· 184 ·

"And so that's okay? If I'd picked some other high school girl, then it would be all right in your book?"

None of this is coming out the way I want it to. "You shouldn't be having sex at all. And never with a teacher. Why don't you get it? Lori used you."

"I didn't feel used. She made me feel good."

"Haven't you been listening to the news reports? All the psychologists they've interviewed? She's damaged you."

He looks disgusted. "Give me a break. Why do I care about a bunch of shrinks' opinions? They're idiots. Everyone wants me to think what Lori and I did was wrong. I don't buy that. Sex feels great. Maybe you should give it a try."

His words hit me like rocks. "I'm not some slut."

His face goes red. "Lori didn't force me. I wanted her."

"So you think that makes it okay? Just because she made you feel good, it was all right? What if it was some male coach at our school doing a girl on a team he controlled? What if he told her she couldn't play unless she put out for him?"

His expression clouds. "That's not the same thing. Lori didn't threaten me. I did it because I wanted to."

"She seduced you, Ryan. She took control of your life and made you do whatever she wanted you to do—cut you off from your friends, made your grades take a nosedive, told you how to spend your time. She turned you into a sneak and a liar. She molded you into what she wanted, not what you wanted."

I see by his face that I've hit home. How could he be so blind to the damage his relationship with Lori did him?

He shakes his head as if to clear it of my arguments. He asks me, "How did you put it together? Where did I slip up?"

"The necklace," I tell him. "I'd seen it in your room and then it was around her neck at the dance. I knew you'd given it to her because it was so unusual and she said it had been a present from a friend. The more I thought about it, the more convinced I became the two of you were . . . together."

He nods. "Yeah, I see how you figured it out. Course, if you hadn't been snooping in my room, you'd never have seen the necklace."

I go hot all over. "I didn't do it on purpose. The box was there in plain view and I opened it."

"I thought you were my friend. I can hardly believe it was you. Hard to believe that you actually searched my computer on purpose."

I hold my head high and look him in the eye. "Yes, I did."

"And then you turned me in. Why did you have to turn us in? I wanted this to happen. I never wanted anything else. The minute I saw Lori, I knew I wanted to be with her. You think it was all her fault. You have no idea. You know nothing about us. Who assigned you to the morality police squad?"

"You were my friend and she was the black widow spider. She was screwing with your head and your life. I don't understand why you don't get that."

He studies me for a minute. His face grows misty because I'm seeing him through a haze of tears. Finally he says, "What do you know, anyway? Well, you don't have to 'protect' me. You never had to. Lori's in jail under suicide watch and I'm not your friend anymore. And you sure as hell aren't mine. Next time you meddle in somebody's life, remember that you leave wreckage behind. You should have minded your own business."

"I couldn't do that with you."

"And why was that, Ms. Goody-goody?"

Because what you did is wrong. Because you kissed me. Because I loved you. Because you broke my heart. "Because I just couldn't."

He shakes his head, gives me a hate-filled look. I watch him turn, open the glass door and walk off into the night.

Ryan

I slip into the botanical gardens when the fog is thick. The bushes are wet and I can hardly make out the colors of the flowers because the mist is so dense. I chose this morning to come here because of the fog. No one else is around. Who visits a garden on a cool, foggy October day? I'm eighteen now, technically all grown up. Even my father thinks of me as grown. He gave me a car when I started my senior year. A long time coming, to my way of thinking.

Dad quit his job and took another one where he doesn't have to travel. He blames himself in part for what happened to me, but we're both in therapy, and according to Dr. Wehrenberg, Dad got so angry because he was supposed to be my "protector." He was supposed to keep me safe, but Lori caught him off guard and made him feel as if he wasn't doing his job as a father. The doc also says that Dad hasn't ever really forgiven Mom for choosing death over staying alive and being married to him.

Therapy is helping Dad, but I'm bored with all the psychobabble, so I sit and nod and pretend I care. Mom killed herself. It happened. Ancient history. I grew up, went after something I wanted. No one seems to get that part.

I pass a clump of yellow mums and on impulse pick several to make a bouquet. I ignore the sign saying DO NOT PICK FLOWERS. I want them and I'm in the habit of taking what I want. No one gets that, either.

Sometimes I think about Honey. She's moved to another neighborhood, and I've heard she's going to some private all-girls school. I never saw her again after that night we talked in her basement, but I'm over being mad at her. Sometimes I miss her—not her, exactly, but the old days when we were kids and hanging out together. She was right about society having a double standard for men and women— the courts are way harder on male teachers who sex it up with girl students than on female teachers who nail guys.

Lori went to jail, but not for long. Turns out that sixteen is the age of consent in Georgia, so the system could only get her for having sex with me when I was fifteen. She got a good lawyer and a sympathetic judge, who was, according to my dad, "an old fart who fell for her good looks," and she only got six months' jail time and nine months' probation and instructions to stay away from me. She can't teach school ever again.

Another thing I've learned is that high school girls who sleep around are considered easy—unless they do it for true love, of course; then it's permissible. But a guy can have sex with lots of girls, without using true love as an excuse, and he's considered experienced. That's the way it's been for me these past two years at school.

I told Dad I wanted to stay at McAllister, and he let me. At first, every time I walked down the hall, heads turned and the whispering started. My attorney and my shrink said "talk to no one," but everyone knows about "that guy Ryan who was nailing his hot teacher." I'm a recovering victim to my teachers, a hero in the eyes of guys at my school, bad-boy attractive to girls who want to try me out. No use wasting good publicity.

I remember telling Lori that she was my first. Girls like hearing that. I don't know why. The truth is, she wasn't my first. The story I told about the girl in the closet was mostly true except for the part about her crying and begging off. She didn't. We went all the way, and I'm telling you, sex inside a cramped closet is no thrill. Not like being with Lori in her bed. There were a couple of others before Lori, but there's no reason to detail them.

A guy has to know how to pick the right girls, though. Zero in on the shy ones, the low-profile and needy ones—except when handed a license by circumstance to take any girl you want. Like the license I was handed when the truth came out about me and Lori. I even hooked up briefly with Jordan Leslie, the senior cheerleading queen on the rebound from Lars.

My dad, my shrink, the cops, the press, all say the same thing about Lori. "She's a predator." "She's a child molester." Can't say I agree, because I don't feel like a victim.

Thinking back, I set out to be seduced by Lori. From the first time I saw her, I wanted to get something going between us. I never thought it would actually happen, but I sure wanted it to. Turned out we both wanted the same thing—each other. I was honked when I found out I wasn't her first boy lover. But I got my head around it after a few sessions with Doc Wehrenberg. I learned that Lori was sexually abused by her father. Her mother knew but didn't protect her. Classic breeding ground for her obsession with young boys, the doc says. "It's about control, not sex," he told me. Whatever.

Doc Wehrenberg also explained that Lori is bipolar—something her attorney used in court to her advantage. She suffers from depression and then swings into manic high gear. I've seen that part with my own eyes. But Lori's taking meds now, and they're supposed to be helping her control her moods.

My shrink believes Lori was a mother substitute in my life. Get real! Lori was hot, beautiful, and I wanted to have sex with her. Sneaking around with her pumped me up and gave me a kind of excitement I'd never had before. Sometimes I think shrinks must have their heads up their butts. I guess Doc Wehrenberg has to tie up all the loose ends to make the pieces fit, but he's not really getting who I am. No one knows the real Ryan, and I'm not about to let my guard down.

I agree with my shrink about one thing, though. In the end it all comes down to power—who has it, who can use it to their advantage to get what they want. Power is everything, and when you have power over someone, it makes you strong and in control.

I wind my way through the foggy paths to the Memory Garden, where statues of nymphs and cherubs line beds of rosebushes. My heart's pounding, wondering if she'll really be here. Then, on a bench far at the back of a place marked CONTEMPLATION AREA, I see her. Her head's covered with a scarf and she's wearing a black coat. Her legs are crossed and she has a book open on her lap. A ruse, I know. She's come to meet me. A risky move on her part, but she's come because I asked her to.

We've been in contact for over a year, but no one knows it. We've exchanged e-mails all this time, but this is our first meeting. I wasn't sure she'd really be here, but when I think about it, she doesn't have anyone else—no family, no friends, no job—and all because of me. Sure, life would be different if I hadn't gotten involved with her, but I did and I'm not one bit sorry. As a bonus, she says she still loves me. Do I love her? Well, I love knowing she needs me. I love knowing I have power and control this time. "Symbiosis"—the interdependence of two separate kinds of organisms. I paid attention in biology, so I recognize it when I see it happening.

Lori tugs her coat more tightly around her. She's cold. I can hardly wait to warm her up. Power surges through me like an electrical charge.

I know what I want. I want Lori. I've wanted her from day one, when she stood in front of our class and our eyes connected. It took months of flirting, talking, sneaking off together to the coffeehouse, participating in special projects, making sure I was always available, before the inevitable happened.

We've been separated for three years now. Lori's been called every detestable name there is. According to the "why don't they mind their own business" experts, I'm still considered a kid, a victim who needs to recover from Lori's sexual exploitation of me. Recover from what? I'm just fine.

In seconds, we'll be together again. It's our destiny. Lori has no one else. She's bound to me, and this time I'll be in the driver's seat. She'll give me anything I want. And I'll make sure she never deserts me. Mom checked out when I was two, but this is about me and Lori and the way she makes me feel, the sense of power I have when I'm with her. I never, ever connected Lori with my mother. Lori was connected to getting my rocks off. She taught me things, did things to me and with me that no high school girl would have done.

Just before I step out of the fog, I relish the fire of anticipation blazing through me, just the way it felt the first time Lori took me to her bed. Watching her through the mist, I can't help wondering—which of us is the predator and which the prey?

A Note from the Author: Part 2

Now you know Ryan and Lori's story. It is fiction, but there are many real relationships like it. The more research I did, the more cases I discovered.

Years can pass before the psychological damage surfaces in a young man's life. One primary long-term effect is the inability of such men to establish lasting relationships with women of a more appropriate age. These men are hesitant to commit, and many suffer from serious depression.

The female teachers who engage in such seductions often have serious emotional problems of their own—histories of physical and sexual abuse, and bipolar or other psychological disorders that contribute to their dysfunctional behavior.

Having studied this growing problem, I have concluded that nothing can justify this kind of relationship. These relationships cause legal, psychological and emotional harm to both parties, as well as to their families and their communities.

The teacher-student relationship has a long and honorable history that society has treasured for generations. From ancient Greece to modern times, the teacher has been a respected professional, and countless students have been nurtured, schooled and launched into the world by men and women who likewise respect and honor their charges. I hold these men and women in the teaching profession in high esteem and trust that they will continue to do the job so many love to do—growing future generations of men and women who will lead this world.

I hope this novel will make you, my readers, think, and help you understand that today you make choices that you will have to live with forever.

Sincerely,

Lurlene McDaniel began writing inspirational novels about teenagers facing life-altering situations when her son was diagnosed with juvenile diabetes. "I saw firsthand how chronic illness affects every aspect of a person's life," she has said. "I want kids to know that while people don't get to choose what life gives to them, they do get to choose how they respond."

Lurlene McDaniel's novels are hard-hitting and realistic, but also leave readers with inspiration and hope. Her books have received acclaim from readers, teachers, parents, and reviewers. Her novels *Don't Die, My Love; I'll Be Seeing You;* and *Till Death Do Us Part* have all been national bestsellers.

Lurlene McDaniel lives in Chattanooga, Tennessee.